NANDINI C SEN teaches ~~~~~~. An erstwhile Fellow at the prestigious Indian Institute of Advanced Study, Shimla, she has received the Charles Wallace Fellowship for Academic Research in London, the Ambassador for Peace Prize for her pioneering work in educating slum dwellers and the Write India award for her creative writing.

Sen writes on Diaspora Studies, African Studies and Comparative Literature. Some of her academic publications include *The Black Woman Speaks: A Study of Flora Nwapa and Buchi Emecheta* (2019), *Through the Diasporic Lens* Volumes 1&2 (2017 & 2018), *Mahasweta Devi: Critical Perspectives* (2012).

Sen is a keen observer of society and a social commentator. Her short stories have been featured in literary journals like *The Elusive Genre* and *The Muse*. She has also been featured in the Asian Collective of Short Stories and the Australia-India collaboration titled *The Glass Walls*.

The Second Wife & Other Stories

Nandini C Sen

Om Books International

First published in 2022 by

Om Books International

Corporate & Editorial Office
A-12, Sector 64, Noida 201 301
Uttar Pradesh, India
Phone: +91 120 477 4100
Email: editorial@ombooks.com
Website: www.ombooksinternational.com

Sales Office
107, Ansari Road, Darya Ganj,
New Delhi 110 002, India
Phone: +91 11 4000 9000
Fax: +91 11 2327 8091
Email: sales@ombooks.com
Website: www.ombooks.com

ISBN: 978-93-91258-95-5

Printed in India

10 9 8 7 6 5 4 3 2 1

Contents

'I can hear the roar of women's silence.'
—Thomas Sankara

For all the women
whose silence speaks louder than words

1

The Sapphire Ring

We tend to co-habit with our past. We allow it to impinge upon our present, our future. Few know how to shrug off a meddlesome past. But I am one such person. If I had allowed my past to spill over into my present, I would not be where I am today. Writing a best-selling novel is one thing, and retaining one's position as a writer of global repute is another. You have to be seen with the right people, make polite chit-chat, issue politically correct statements, air-kiss and hug your tribe, sign up for endless quid pro quos—it is all part of the game. Over the years, I have learnt to deal my cards well, and have come up trumps.

Never for a moment mistake me to be a man given to self-praise. Quite the contrary, I am extremely self-critical at times. But today, I feel self-indulgent. They are considering my name for the Moon Brooks, the prestigious literary prize, and if Sara is to be believed, I am the next winner.

The jury has long mastered the art of juggling Whites, Browns, Blacks and Yellows skilfully. This time, they are determined to pick someone from South Asia. And Sara, my lucky charm, has already nudged the right people in the right places.

***

The key turned noisily in the lock and I heard Sara's impatient footsteps on the carpeted floor. Bruno, my sole companion for years, cocked his ears at the sounds and then curled himself up on the rug and went back to sleep. He was used to Sara being around.

Sara and I had been together for nearly five years. Born to a German mother and a Sindhi father, she was strikingly beautiful, and had inherited her mother's chiselled features and her father's innate business sense. An extremely successful literary agent, she was known for making or breaking literary careers.

She had breezed into my life at a writer's meet in Delhi. That fateful evening, we had chatted over cocktails and, later, found ourselves making passionate love in her hotel room. What drew her to me is anyone's guess. Oftentimes, she would say jokingly that I reminded her of her favourite uncle. Anyway, I was old enough to be one.

Sara is eighteen years younger to me and fiercely independent. She has refused to move in with me. She comes and goes as she pleases. Her love making is as unpredictable as she is. Of late, I have started depending entirely on her advice for my writing. The ideas and thoughts are hers, and I put them into words just as the love making is initiated by her and I simply play along.

Today, Sara has come to my apartment during her lunch break. I think she is just what Bruno and I need—a hiatus from our humdrum routine. She says she will spend an hour with me before meeting a client.

I busy myself getting lunch organised while she sits in the kitchen going through her notes. Bruno wags his tail in delight and snuggles up close to her. She strokes his head affectionately with her perfectly manicured fingers. Sometimes, I envy the ease with which Bruno demands attention and gets it. I try to not meet Sara's eyes. She is too much of a distraction—every part of my body is aroused in her presence.

'Ru, have you ever thought of writing about the Naxalbari movement?' Sara asks while peering at her papers.

The soup spoon falls from my hand into the bowl with a clatter.

She looks up and stares at me with those piercing eyes. 'Ru, you were a student in Kolkata in the '60s and '70s. You would've seen things first hand. Why don't you write about your experiences?'

I mutter an inadequate answer.

Soon it is time for her to leave. She kisses me on the mouth and is bewildered at my tepid reaction. Does she sense anything? She pats Bruno goodbye. 'You have become as lazy as your master. Take care, both of you.' She smiles at me as she closes the door behind her.

I am unable to meet her eyes. My mind is a blur of images. The floodgates of memory burst open and hold me hostage, like a film playing out in a confused sequence. The present and past merge in a bizarre canvas as I sit at my study table. The desktop screen comes alive; out of sheer habit, my fingers start to play the keyboard. I don't intend to write the story, the one about three people—Raghab Banerjee, Geeta Lahiri and me, Raghab's younger brother Rutajeet, but something seems to wrest it out of me.

Years step aside, and I am back on the streets of Kolkata. Amidst a mass boycott of classes, the students have taken out a protest march. Raghab is at the head, shouting anti-government slogans. I don't care about Raghab's political leanings, but I join the march because of Geeta. I have loved her for as long as I can remember. She is my classmate in Presidency College, majoring in English. Tall and simple, Geeta wears a white sari with a dark blue border. Her hair is bunched together in two waist-length plaits. The only piece of jewellery she wears is a sapphire ring which sparkles each time she raises her fisted hand in protest. As the march moves along the bylanes of Kolkata, I try to move closer to Geeta.

'Haven't you had enough of this? Can we go to the Coffee House for some time?' I ask her.

Geeta raises her eyebrows, ignores me and carries on with greater determination. She is now close to Raghab and raises her fist in solidarity with him. Raghab looks at her and smiles.

I am overcome with anger. 'Raghab and Geeta? No, no,' I assure myself. 'She loves me. She must be doing this to make me jealous.'

The march moves through the area, punctuated by the rhythmic chant of 'Lal Salam' and 'Land to the Tiller'.

The unrest in Kolkata is growing worse. Colleges have shut down. The students' revolt has now taken on a far larger dimension. The student community has vowed to stand by the tillers of the land and fight for their right to the land. It has become a mass struggle where students from elite colleges, farmers, Santhals and other marginalised groups are standing together and demanding equal status for all. The students have relocated to the villages to 'give politics' to the farmers, all under the orders of the High Command of the Movement.

The government has retaliated with all its might. Young boys are being dragged out of their homes and murdered in cold blood. But repression is hardly a deterrent; the students are determined to risk their all for the rights of their less-privileged brothers and sisters.

***

Two weeks back, Raghab disappeared under the cover of darkness. The police landed up home and took charge. Every part of the house was searched, and finally Raghab's room sealed, to contain a contagion, as it were.

Thereafter, Geeta and I met frequently. We were aware of being watched closely by the police, so we chose to play safe. We found answers to our silent questions in each other's eyes. Geeta was easy to get along with. Being voracious readers, we bonded over books. We pretended everything was fine, and Raghab would be back soon. My heart would jump with joy on seeing her. Her simplicity and grace had such a hold on me, I could do anything for her.

Then one day, Geeta did not show up. I dashed across to her house only to discover it was locked. I asked around frantically, but no one knew anything about her. I went numb with shock. Where could she possibly be? Then with a sinking heart, I realised she too had probably gone 'underground'.

In the days that followed, sinister murmurs did the rounds: 'The whore will be found and killed.' 'What kind of a girl brings such shame to her family?'

I muttered to myself over and over again, 'She is innocent. Please don't punish her. Please don't.'

Every so often, I was hauled off to the police station and asked the same questions—at times politely, at times violently and on the odd occasion, after a brutal round of thrashing. My answers never varied—I truly knew nothing about Raghab or Geeta. They had chosen to keep me in the dark. Perhaps I was too young...or too fickle.

Then the police struck a deal.

I went from one village to another in search of them. Deep down, I knew Raghab and Geeta were together. One day, in a sleepy little town in Bihar, I spotted Geeta in the marketplace with some village women. Though she was dressed like them, her face partially covered with her sari, I recognised her instantly. I followed her at a safe distance back to her refuge. When night fell, I decided to speak with her. The farmer's family that sheltered her denied she was with them. After a heated argument, Geeta emerged from the house. She didn't seem surprised to see me. One would think she was expecting me.

'Let him in, please. He is Raghab's brother.'

I could not bear to look at her face. She had tanned beyond recognition. Her hair was matted and unruly.

'What have you done to yourself? Where is Raghab? Why did you run away without telling me?'

We talked late into the night. She told me about her current portfolio—educating agrarian women and training them for a mass movement that was to follow. Raghab, despite his indifferent health, lived far away in another village where he was mobilising the farming youth.

I asked her to come away with me, but she laughed off my suggestion. Instead, she made me promise to return to Kolkata. 'And you shall not tell anyone about our whereabouts,' she added before bidding me goodbye with a smile.

***

I did exactly as the police had asked me to. Raghab was apprehended and tried in the court. I testified against him, my own brother. He accepted the charges with his characteristic smile. Before being whisked away to jail, he wished to talk to me alone. He smiled while handing me a packet. 'Give it to her,' he said, as if nothing had changed between us.

I had tears in my eyes. What had I done? Betrayed my own blood? But Raghav just smiled,' It's okay, Khokon,' he said, gently patting my back. 'Take good care of her.'

That was my arrangement with the police. Geeta would never get to know of it. She would return to Kolkata. No charges would be pressed against her. I would sell my property and get the best lawyers for Raghab. I would convince her I would fight tooth and nail to free Raghab, but, temporarily, we would have to leave the city. I would do all this for her, but she would have to agree to be mine.

The day I was supposed to meet Geeta, I was extremely nervous. In my head, I had rehearsed all the answers to the questions she was likely to ask.

***

She did not cry nor did she give in to histrionics. All she asked was, 'Did he give you anything for me?'

I handed over the packet to her.

She opened it and pulled out her sapphire ring. Her face broke into a childlike smile as she slipped the ring on her finger. 'Thank you, Rutajeet. Now, please leave me alone,' she said. 'And yes, you would do well to leave the city early tomorrow morning. As an elder brother, Raghab may have forgiven you, but his friends won't.'

Her icy voice chilled me to the bone.

***

Geeta surrendered to the police. I would learn of it from the local dailies. The very next day, I left Kolkata for good. I never heard of her again.

A year later, it was reported that the dreaded Naxal Raghab Banerjee had tried to escape from jail. The police had shot him dead at point-blank range. It was my cue to leave the country.

A few odd jobs here and there, and I was finally able to find my calling as a writer.

***

It's late in the evening. Since the last few hours, I have not moved from my table. I breathe in spurts as though I were relearning to breathe. My fingers wind down their dance on the keyboard and become still. I no longer want to type. The world should never unearth my deepest secret.

Stop. Stop.

But my fingers no longer heed my command.

I break into a sweat. Bruno senses something is amiss and cries out for help, as though he were human.

The keyboard swims in front of my eyes. I make a desperate attempt to find the delete button, but in vain.

My last thoughts before I slip into nothingness are of the beautiful Geeta leading the march, her long plaits swinging to her gait and her sapphire ring blazing in the sun.

2

Nabonita

Nabonita was no good at stealing. Being an only child, she had been well taken care of. She had had no dearth of food, so, stealing even tidbits from the kitchen, which all her friends did, was alien to her. But today, she would have to steal and hide something. She would have to walk all the way from the kitchen to her bedroom hiding it in the folds of her sari. The mere thought sent a chill up her spine. She could feel its sharp edge against her body as she pictured herself carrying it to her bed. Nabonita was sure her heartbeat was echoing across the house. She could be caught any moment now and yet she knew she had to do it.

***

Her father Jochan worked in one of the burgeoning factories in Asansol. He was a man of modest means, but for Nabo, he had dared to dream. Much to the amazement of his colleagues, he had sent her to a well-known missionary school. 'You want your only child to be a Taansh Firangi Christian?' they had asked.

Jochan's boss had not been amused. He thought Jochan had deliberately insulted him by daring to enroll his daughter in the same school where his children studied. Jochan bore all the insults quietly as secretly he nursed the desire to see his daughter rub shoulders with the elite. Having worked as a clerk all his life, he had divined the key to success. You had to know how to speak English and to this end, he was happy spending a fortune sending his daughter to an elite school.

His wife Maya was convinced that Jochan was insane. Unable to rile against him openly, she fixed the blame on her dead mother-in-law. 'She comes in his dream and feeds him all this madness. Whoever heard of a girl going to an English medium school?' Maya would complain to anyone who cared to listen. She would bemoan the day her marriage had been solemnised, the evil stars under which the girl was born and above all, the machinations of her dead mother-in-law who managed to influence her husband even from the grave.

Nabo, however, remained unfazed by such goings-on around her. She was aware of her father daring to dream above his station and her mother's desire for a boy child, but that did not spoil her childhood. She would help her father draft letters in English, and laugh at her mother's belief about her grandmother's visitations and try to make her understand that no such thing was possible.

Nabo was reasonably good at studies and when a 'foreign' lady in white headgear and habit talked to Maya in Bangla about her daughter, Maya felt reassured. The 'foreign' lady was an Anglo-Indian nun who had been born in Kolkata, but to Maya, she seemed to belong to another planet. Slowly she came around to thinking that Jochan had done something right. Maybe Nabo was shaping up well. The Mothers and Sisters at the missionary school were nice to Nita, who managed reasonably well to walk the tightrope between being Nabo at home and Nita at school.

Maya was happy with the school and what they were teaching her daughter, particularly when Nabo reached puberty. She did not need her mother's help and was able to manage things on her own. That bit was good, but the problem arose when Maya asked her daughter to step out of the kitchen, to not sit on a chair, to not touch the jar of pickle, and so on. Nabo rebelled. Jochan was not allowed to participate in this discussion. It was entirely between mother and daughter. Their argument became so shrill pitched that Nabo refused to talk to her mother. Maya resorted to the only tricks in her bag—cry out to her gods, rile against her dead mother-in-law and lament her cursed fate.

One day, a letter arrived. Maya's elder sister Sandhya and her husband Bratibabu would visit them the coming Saturday, and stay for lunch. For Jochan and Maya, this was no less than a royal visit. The couple forgot their differences and set about preparing to receive their special guests. Jochan borrowed some money from his colleague and bought a variety of fish—pabda, ilish and chingri. He wondered whether this would be enough. Maya needed Nabo's help and so the girl was back in the kitchen. However, she warned Nabo against airing her new-fangled ideas in front of Mashimoni and Meshomoshay.

Mashimoni was much older than Nabo's mother, and had been married off in her teens to a rich businessman who owned a palatial house in South Kolkata. Their only son was settled in the US and visited them occasionally. He had been 'ensnared' by an American woman, but that was not to be discussed in the family in deference to their standing in society. Rumour had it that the daughter-in-law had visited them only once and never returned.

Meshomoshay belonged to a Kulin Kayastha family that was known to have donated generously to the freedom movement. Tall and fair-skinned, he wore a sparkling white dhoti at home and a Park Circus-tailored suit for his business meetings. Mashimoni was petite, slim and fair and the sindoor in the parting of her grey hair was bright red. Maya could not help but endlessly repeat to Jochan that each silk sari worn by her sister cost more than what he earned in an entire year. Quiet by nature, Jochan held his tongue. Secretly, he had always been in awe of this part of his wife's family and now Maya was asking Jochan to consult the formidable Bratibabu on Nabo's future. He would be the right person to advise them on this wayward girl's marriage. He would also be able to help financially since he did not have a daughter of his own.

'Don't forget to propose that Jamaibabu should perform the kanyadaan,' Maya instructed Jochan. Giving away a girl in marriage was considered an extremely pious act by the Hindus and to bestow Bratibabu the honour might mean that he would take an active interest in the girl's future. Maya pinned all her hopes on the lunch she would organise for her sister and brother-in-law. She would serve them to the best of her ability to ensure her daughter would be married into a rich household. That could happen if Bratibabu took things into his own hands.

Royalty arrived on Saturday. Nabo had never met her aunt and uncle before. She touched their feet and sought their blessings. Her aunt commented approvingly on her demure looks, the prim and proper salwar kameez she wore and her oiled and braided hair replete with red ribbons tied in bows. The white of her uncle's starched dhoti and the brightness of her aunt's sari blinded her. As their driver brought the gifts inside the house, for the first time, Nabo realised what it felt to be a poor relation.

Her house and her parents shrank before her eyes. With their upmarket Kolkata air, her uncle and aunt mesmerised her. When the meal was served, Nabo was acutely conscious of its inadequacy even though her uncle and aunt were gracious and praised every dish. Finally, as Bratibabu belched, washed his hands on his plate and dried it on the gamchha which Jochan held out for them, Maya broached the topic of her daughter. Nabo had been asked to go out of the room on the pretext of fetching paan, but she stood at the door, hearing every word that her mother spoke.

Maya talked about her wretched middle-class existence and her daughter's fate. With pride, she recounted Nabo's progress in school and added hastily that it wouldn't count for much in the marriage market. Bratibabu was rich and powerful. If he and Didi took pity on their Nabo, she might have a better future.

Nabo held her breath. Her heart beat wildly in her chest as if she were awaiting her school results. The frog in the well suddenly had a fleeting glimpse of the ocean. Nabo's entire being was now focussed on a single prayer: 'Please God, make them say yes. Make them take me to Kolkata.'

She was shaken out of her reverie when someone uttered her name. It was Bratibabu. 'Don't stand at the door, Ma. Come here. I need to talk to you.'

Embarrassed at being caught eavesdropping, Nabo walked towards him like a petty criminal, but he was quick to put her at ease.

'We are discussing your future. You should be here.'

Touched by his magnanimity, she wowed to do everything to make her aunt and uncle proud of her. He made her sit next to him and encouraged her to talk. She told them about her school, the Mother Superior, her role as a singer in the school choir. It was as if the floodgates of a young heart had been thrown open. Nabo continued to talk and her uncle listened, coaxing her gently to reveal more about herself. She found herself telling him about how her parents called her Nabo while at school they called her Nita. There! Her biggest secret had been divulged—the tightrope she walked between the two worlds. Nabo and Nita— Nabonita—were the same person.

Her uncle laughed. 'Well, from today I will give you a special name too. I will call you Bonny.'

'Bonny?'

'Yes Bonny—someone who is pretty, and you my dear are very pretty indeed!'

Nabo's cup of happiness brimmed over. She also learnt that she was the namesake of a distinguished Bengali professor and writer. Her respect for her uncle increased manifold. Not only was he a man of wealth, but he was also a man of letters. She could never converse with her father like this, nor with her mother for that matter. Within hours, Nabo was ready to sever ties with her humdrum parents and with her modest house in Asansol. She was set to fly to Kolkata where she knew a great future awaited her.

Only nobody said a word about her going anywhere.

Lunch over, Bratibabu and Sandhya stood up to take leave. The family of three touched their feet in reverence. Nabo felt let down. All this conversation, and her being renamed Bonny had come to naught. She would remain trapped in this miserable existence for the rest of her life. As she bent to touch her uncle's feet, he held her chin and tilted her face up gently towards him in paternal benevolence.

'Bonny will stay with us after she finishes school. I will send her to college in Kolkata. Why talk of marriage so soon? Many more offers will come her way if she is college-educated.'

Nabo's eyes filled with tears of gratitude.

That night, Maya shed tears of joy. God had finally heeded her prayers. Her daughter would not suffer like her. She would prosper like her elder sister. Bratibabu was sure to find a great match for Nabo.

Jochan remained quiet. All these years of toiling and caring for his only child meant nothing to Nabo; she was ready to distance herself from them. Well, if that brought her prosperity and happiness, so be it...

***

Years went by. The quiet Nabo turned garrulous. She talked about going to college in Kolkata, something few of her classmates could boast of. Every year on her birthday, a parcel arrived from her uncle and aunt. New salwar kameezes—way more fashionable than what girls wore in these parts, bangles to match and some money in an envelope. With her newfound riches, she acquired a fashionable haircut. Jochon was aghast, but now Nabo had a new ally—her mother supported her in whatever she did.

Nabo spoke rudely to her father whom both mother and daughter dubbed a loser. As always, Jochan took this humiliation too in his stride. If this was good for his child, he was willing to step back and let her fly.

And fly she did indeed to Kolkata as her uncle's car picked her up from Howrah Station and headed to their palatial house in Ballygunge.

***

Nabo had wept, embracing her mother who kept wiping her tears with her aanchal. Jochan had cried like a baby as his daughter left with her two escorts. Bratibabu had taken care of her travel. He had discouraged her parents from accompanying her. He had sent two middle-aged people—a man and a woman who travelled with her by train and later by car.

Nabo's eyes may have been moist, but Jochan could see in them the excitement of inhabiting a new world. With all his heart, he wished her well. He prayed to the Almighty for his only child's well-being. Maya was convinced that her daughter was poised to take off into the world of riches and glamour.

Many times in her mind Nabo had gone over her grand arrival at the palatial home in Kolkata. She imagined that the house she had heard so much about but never seen before, had already become *her* home. She had visions of her aunt rushing out to embrace her, with her uncle in tow. She saw the servants standing by to welcome the young, new mistress of the house. Isn't that what her mother had told her? 'They don't have a daughter. The daughter-in-law is a firangi and doesn't stay there. Didi is getting old. So, effectively you will be the new mistress of the house.'

As she entered from the kachari, her uncle barely looked up. Somehow, he looked much older and more distant than the man she remembered having met in Asansol. Her aunt, free from the glamour of the silk sari and clad in a cotton nightgown, seemed to have shrunk. She was, however, hospitable and showed Nabo to her room. She also conveyed to her the rules of the household.

Nabo would have to wake up early, make her own bed and help in the kitchen. She would be escorted to college by a servant and would have to be back by noon. After that, there would be endless chores; she was expected to keep herself occupied. At no time was she to be seen conversing with men. She would have to be demurely clad in salwar kameezes or saris and her hair would have to be tied. Her aunt did not approve of the haircut.

A stunned Nabonita tried to adapt to her new life. The college in Kolkata was nothing like she had imagined. Girls sashayed around in outlandish outfits. Men and women hung around in coffee houses where laughter mixed with cigarette smoke hung thick in the air. They knew so much, discussed so many things that Nabo retreated into her own shell. She wanted to show off her new name—she would be 'Bonny' to friends. Instead, she ended up in the lonely corner of her class, shrinking into oblivion. In spite of her uncle and aunt's strange demeanour, she preferred the house to her life outside. The day was fraught with innumerable chores, but Nabo did not mind doing these. She had spent her childhood years helping her mother.

The maids in the house who had earlier seemed hostile now warmed up to this girl. They talked to her about their poverty-stricken life which had forced them to come to this merciless city. About Nabo, they wondered why any parent would let their only child lead such an existence in this strange, rich man's abode? The maids saw in Nabo a companion and she started to feel at ease with them. Her aunt remained busy, participating in numerous social causes for which she had to travel across the city. Her uncle, she barely saw. It seemed the man who had mesmerised her in Asansol had completely vanished.

Only at night, when Nabonita retreated to her tiny room, would she dare to be her old self again. She would let her hair down and indulge in flights of fantasy in the letters she sent home. 'College was fun,' she would bluff, 'as is the house where I am the cynosure of Meshomoshay and Mashimoni's eyes.' She told them that the maids bowed to her out of respect as did the driver who drove her to college. The girls in the college were envious of her new dresses and stunning hairdos.

Maya shed tears of happiness as she read the letters aloud to her husband. Jochan tried to sound happy too, but a strange worry for his only child gnawed away at his soul. Of course, Nabo had categorically discouraged them from visiting the Kolkata house.

Days rolled into months. From being the beloved daughter of her parents, Nabo now became a pale shadow of the person she once had been. Not being academically inclined, college failed to hold any charm for her. Her only release came from the letters she wrote, creating imaginary oases in her desert-like existence.

One day, she learnt from the maids that her aunt would be travelling to Burdwan for a meeting. She would be gone for two nights and preparations were on for the impending trip. Her aunt gave instructions to the cook and the kitchen help. There were no special instructions for Nabo other than the usual stuff—she was to behave properly, dress modestly, not stay out late or go flirting around with men, and so on. Seema, the elderly cook was tasked to keep an eye on her.

Though Nabo had had very little interaction with her aunt, she still heaved a sigh of relief. To celebrate her freedom, she decided to not go to college and to stay with the maids in the kitchen instead. The maids were quite happy to have an extra helping hand. In the evening, she retreated early into her room and lay on the bed reading. Not being much of a reader, the book soon slipped from her hand and she dozed off.

Suddenly Nabo woke up to the strange sensation of a hand groping her waist. As she tried to scream, a hand cupped her mouth. She tried to scream again but her voice was muffled. Then an urgent but caring voice spoke to her, 'It's me child. Relax. Don't be afraid.'

Nabo was certain she was in the midst of a nightmare when she distinctly heard Bratibabu's voice repeat what she had heard before. 'Bonny, it's me. Now, be a good girl. Just relax.'

A stunned Nabo lay still like a paralysed rag doll, unable to understand what was happening. Bratibabu's experienced hand ran over her body, coaxing her to respond. He cupped her breasts, and kissed her on the mouth repeatedly. He undid the drawstrings of her salwar, rubbing her hard till she was sore.

At her utter lack of response, the hands which had been gentle so far were now rough as was his mouth offending. He bit her and mauled her while his body ravaged hers. He flung her all over the bed and the floor like a hapless prey... And then suddenly, it was over...as if nothing had happened. Even if Nabo had wanted to believe this was just a bad dream, the drops of blood on her bed, the bite marks on her breast and the searing pain between her legs confirmed that her life had changed forever.

Seema, the elderly maid who had been instructed to keep an eye on Nabo carried her food to the room. She was gentle as she helped Nabo from the bed to the mora on which she sat down gingerly to eat her food. Not a word was exchanged between the two, but Nabo knew she had a sympathiser in the house. Seema picked up the soiled sheets and left the room.

The following night, Nabo pleaded with her, 'Please stay with me, Mashi.'

'I can't, dear,' was all Seema said.

Nabo stayed awake. A million things were passing through her head. Her uncle—the respected Mr. Bratiraj Datta Chaudhury—had raped her. What if she were already pregnant or infected with some deadly disease. How would she deal with all this? Who would believe her story? How would she escape from this house and if at all she did, would she be able to face her parents?

Then Bratibabu walked in. This time, there was no preamble—no attempt at conversation. Nabo was surprised at her own reaction. Instead of rebelling, her body just gave in. This pleased Bratibabu enormously. The biting and mauling lessened. He said she was very beautiful. He said he would take care never to impregnate her. It was only by being his special woman that she would learn how to pleasure her future husband.

Nabo's life fell into a strange pattern. She withdrew into herself. She gave up the pretence of pursuing academics completely. All day long, she would sit in her room brooding. The letters to her parents stopped even though her aunt insisted she keep up the drill or else her parents would start to worry. Sometimes, Seema would come in to oil and braid her hair. She would talk constantly while Nabo stared blankly at the floor.

She was not his only girl. 'Kartababu', as Seema addressed Bratibabu, was known for his weakness for women. He had not spared the women of his own family—the main reason why his son and his wife never visited them again. His younger sister had committed suicide when she was barely in her twenties. Kartama (his wife) had suffered much at his hands and now preferred to keep him happy by providing him with pretty young and pliable women.

Nabo was shaken to the core. So Mashimoni had been party to this all along! That was why Nabo had been plucked from her house in Asansol.

Bratibabu was careful not to enter Nabo's room when his wife was home, but Mashimoni had started to travel quite often. Nabo was convinced that this was deliberate. She learnt to switch off her mind and gave in to Bratibabu's whims. Gifts followed in the form of silk saris and priceless jewellery. Being the master's mistress earned her immense power in the Datta Chaudhury household. She was now treated with some degree of respect even by her aunt.

When she finally did start writing to her parents, her letters were brief and impersonal. She shunned human company and preferred to remain in her room. Outwardly, she was respectful to both her aunt and uncle, but something within her had snapped. Nabo did not recognise herself anymore. In her mind, she kept looking for ways to escape—perhaps she could run away on the pretext of going to college. But running away did not seem a likely solution. The Datta Chaudhurys were extremely well connected. She would be dragged right back into this hell hole.

Then one day, an idea struck her. It was the only
way she could reclaim herself. At first, the very thought
of it made her shiver and she fell ill. It took her a few
days to recover, but the thought had taken root within
her. As she mulled over it, a plan began to evolve. It
would require every bit of daring she possessed, but it
had to be done. She needed to feel whole again.

***

The kitchen was relatively empty in the evening as most
of the cooking was done in the morning. Yet, Seema
stayed put well after dinner had been served. It was
her duty to take warm milk to Kartababu's study, after
which she would latch the kitchen door and turn in.
On days when Bratibabu wished to spend his evenings
drinking whiskey, the milk would remain untouched.
In a mock show of concern for her husband's health,
Mashimoni would scold him for not finishing it. It
would then be poured into the bowl for the cats.

Nabo knew she would have to enter the kitchen
during the brief period when Seema went to the study.
The kitchen door creaked and any attempt to open it
after it had been latched was sure to rouse suspicion.

She planned every move meticulously. This would
mean the end of her life, but she couldn't care less.

She knew the Datta Chaudhurys would not spare her parents. They would be hauled over the coals. But even her love for her parents was not going to stop her now. For the first time in years, Nabonita felt truly alive. She had a mission to accomplish.

On the appointed day, as Nabonita bathed and dressed, she could see a mad glint in her eyes. She was sure people were staring at her. Her guilt-laden face was sure to give her away. The day, however, passed sans incident. To show everything was normal, she forced herself to eat her dinner. Soon, it was time for Seema to carry the glass of milk down the corridor for Kartababu. This was the opportunity Nabonita had been looking for. She made a dash for the kitchen.

***

Bratibabu remembered the time when he had first met Nabo. He knew he had to have her, but had decided to give her time to grow up. A young girl would give her all to her benefactor and Bratibabu had entered her life before anyone else had. He was convinced he was her first love and slowly, he would mould her entirely to his liking. He wished he could do more for her—take her to the cinema and the like, but given his station in life, that was not possible.

His chest puffed up in self-importance. He hailed from a distinguished family, but he had not rested on his laurels. The love and respect he earned from the ruling Party was because of his sustained efforts at keeping the Party coffers ringing. All this could not be compromised for this chit of a girl.

Slowly and steadily he walked towards her room. She was in there, standing still. Bratibabu noticed that she had not changed out of her sari.

He had bought her so many lacey nightgowns, but this girl still carried on with her small-town habits. A nasty comment rose to his lips which he stifled. No point spoiling the evening. He walked up to her and held her in his arms. How tiny she is. I need to feed her up a bit, he thought. He continued to kiss her on the mouth as he led her towards the bed. Slowly, Nabo extricated herself and helped him lie down.

'Good. She is learning,' he thought as he closed his eyes in sweet anticipation. His dhoti had come undone and his manhood stood erect as he lay back, letting the young girl take the lead. Occasionally, he liked that. She was a good learner. Suddenly, he felt something hard, sharp and steely pressing against his neck. At first, he ignored it, but then it started to cut into his skin.

'Bonny!' he tried to call out. But there she was standing next to him, pressing the sharp edge of the

bothi against his throat. He shut his eyes willing the
nightmare to pass but the pain was unbearable.

'Bratibabu,' Nabonita spoke in a clear voice.

Shocked that she had dared to call him by his
name, he realised he had never heard her voice—he
had never needed to. She continued to speak while
he lay unmoving, lest the blade penetrate deeper
into his neck.

Nabonita continued, 'I could kill you right away,
but that would not be punishment enough for you.
Your sister's suicide case is still pending in court and if
you feel no one will testify against you, well, the driver
will speak, as will Seema. The maids in the kitchen are
only too willing to provide detailed accounts of your
debauchery. And if any further evidence is required,
your daughter-in-law is willing to step in.'

Bratibabu doubled up in pain. Nabonita could not
be bothered. She had chosen her weapon well. This
bothi's blade was sharpened regularly. In the Datta
Chaudhury household, this bothi had cut and shaped
several kinds of fish and vegetables, but this was the
first time it had drawn human blood.

She had made a deep cut in his neck. Blood oozed
from the fresh wound as she watched unperturbed.
Then she withdrew the bothi from the gash in his
neck, straightened her sari, adjusted the aanchal and

walked towards the kitchen. The door creaked open, but Nabonita was no longer scared of anyone in this household. She placed the blood-smeared bothi back from where she had taken it. Quietly and purposefully she walked out, shutting the kitchen door behind her.

The night was dark and still. Not a single watchman was in sight. The deathly silence was punctuated by the occasional chirping of crickets as Nabo exited the massive wrought-iron gates of the Datta Chaudhury mansion. Her hands were still warm from the touch of the bothi's killer blade. Every word she had spoken to Bratibabu had been a lie, but she had dared and won that decisive round.

Unafraid, Nabonita pulled her sari tightly around her frail body, and continued walking briskly on the cobbled streets of the unfamiliar city.

3

The Performer

Sameer, Tiya, Tathya and Nira—their photographs were neatly mounted on the living room wall of a sprawling bungalow in the burgeoning metropolis of Gurgaon. Nira holding Tiya to her bosom when the latter was all of two months; cutting Tathya's birthday cake with him as he turned eleven; her and Sameer's wedding photographs—Nira looking bashful, her eyes lowered and Sameer proud and smiling. The wall depicted a happy and smiling urban family.

Sameer had come into Nira's life through a family friend. An engineer working in Germany, he was considered an eligible bachelor in her parents' circle of friends. Nira had just completed her graduation. Their parents were quick to formalise the marriage and in no time, Nira found herself in a cold, alien land with very little to occupy her. She coped by remaining connected to her friends and family through the countless letters and photo albums she sent home. The smiling photographs of the duo in the beautiful locales of Germany bore testimony to their 'happily married' status. To her friends and family in India, she seemed to be living the charmed dream of every young girl whose idea of marriage is fashioned by Bollywood. Nira kept up the illusion of the happy marriage, masking her loneliness well.

A year into their marriage, Nira's father was diagnosed with lung cancer. Being an only child, it was imperative she be with him. She went on to nurse him for six long months before he passed away. Sameer cooperated with Nira, albeit grudgingly. He found a job in India and moved back after four months of their being apart. However, he would never let Nira forget what a huge sacrifice he had made in terms of his career by moving back to India. It hung like a sword between the couple for years though outwardly they carried on as if everything was normal.

They chose to settle down at Nira's parents' place as her mother was finding it difficult to manage the house on her own. Soon her mother retreated into her pooja room, relieved that her daughter and son-in-law were around to take care of her house and property. Two years later, just before Tiya's birth, she left them forever. Tiya was extra-special to Nira as the elders in the family assured her that her mother had been reborn as her daughter.

Sameer behaved like a reasonably good husband and slowly, Nira was able to cast off the sadness that had overcome her after her parents' demise. Soon, she became pregnant again. This time, she was more confident about the impending childbirth, but Sameer did not share her excitement. It dampened her spirits, but Nira tried to stay happy through her pregnancy. Soon Tathya their son was born and Sameer seemed happy again. Later, he confided in her that he had been apprehensive about having another daughter. Nira was furious and hurt, but she let it pass. Over time, she relegated it to standard Indian male insensitivity. She would also tell herself that it was a one-off comment and he had not really meant it. If he had anything against girls, would he continue to dote on Tiya?

Nira's in-laws were a reticent and quiet couple who preferred to live in their ancestral house in Mysore. Rarely did they visit Gurgaon nor did they insist on their son visiting them. Sameer went to see them occasionally, but never insisted on Nira and the children going with him. As the children turned into teenagers, the visits to Mysore became a thing of the past. Now the children planned the vacations and the family travelled to exotic locations within and outside the country. Life seemed to have treated Nira well. She was the focal point of her household. Though her family did not thank her for it, Nira knew they could not manage a single day without her.

Nira's hands were always full—taking her daughter for her physics tuitions and ballet classes; taking her son for his tennis and cricket lessons, and ensuring the driver, cook and maid came to work on time. Sameer had recently developed a cholesterol problem, so the food had to be cooked in less oil. The cook would never get it right, so she had to be in the kitchen to instruct her. Sameer had risen through the ranks at his workplace and was expected to host some office parties at home. Nira would plan the parties for days; the house would be decorated accordingly, and appropriate gifts would be bought for the guests, Sometimes, she would feel totally drained at the end of the day.

To ease her cervical problem, she started to take yoga lessons. Having been an avid reader in the past, she still carried a book to bed, but as soon as her exhausted head hit the pillow, she would be fast asleep. Very often, Sameer would gently remove her glasses and close the book as she turned on her side and drifted into a deep slumber. Sameer teased her that she snored sometimes though Nira refused to believe it. She had also started to put on some weight. Her waist had thickened, and her breasts had started to sag. However, Nira had adjusted to her middle-aged self and did very little to camouflage her age. Sameer did not seem to have a problem and she did not have the time to care. Life was a roller-coaster ride and Nira struggled hard to be a good mother, wife and homemaker.

One evening, as Nira sat at Tathya's cricket academy fanning herself and praying his coaching would be over soon, he rushed to her, panting, saying 'sir' wanted to have a word with her. Sensing a fee hike was in order, Nira stood up with great reluctance. She frowned at Javed Sir who stood before her, his hands folded in namaste. A tall, rugged and unkempt man, he was wiping his sweat with an alarmingly yellowing handkerchief. Nira took a few steps back and almost held her breath lest she smell his body odour. Javed didn't seem to notice.

'Madam, he needs a new bat. Please buy him a "cheapanbest" one.'

'Kya? What?' Nira looked confused.

'Mom, he means cheap and best,' decoded Tathya, staring at the floor and not meeting his mother's eyes. Nira nodded. Later, mother and son collapsed with laughter the minute they got into their car.

'How do you understand what he says?' Neera asked amidst guffaws.

'Mom, he is a good coach. He speaks to us in Hindi. I don't know why he was trying to speak to you in English.'

Nira started to meet Javed quite often. Tathya was performing well and Javed had started to take a personal interest in him. The mother was often called for consultation and Nira found herself at the cricket institute most days of the week. Javed would sit with her sometimes while Tathya did his net practice. He also had a helper who followed the boys around at practice. Nira had got over her initial awkwardness with Javed. They would talk while watching Tathya continue with his practice sessions.

'Madam, I'm not very educated. Can you please teach me some English?' Javed said one day. Upon enquiry, Nira found out that Javed belonged to one of the villages adjoining Gurgaon. Though located just a few kilometres away from the metropolis, his part of the world was a semi-rural set-up. He had passed his higher secondary examination from a local school and was now pursuing his graduation through a distance learning course.

'Madam, here no one thinks anything of me, but back home, I am seen as an achiever. I have invested

some money in this academy. I send money to my
parents and I am also saving for my sister's marriage,'
Javed told Nira.

At first, Nira's response to Javed was polite and
impersonal. As their encounters grew more frequent,
she thought of him as a 'simple and nice person' and
would hear him out with some degree of indulgence.

***

Summer was at its peak and the school vacations had
started. Sameer was tied up at work, so there was no
vacation in the offing for the family. Tathya was becoming
increasingly passionate about cricket, so Nira was forced
to go to the academy with him almost every day of the
week. Her friends from the kitty group encouraged her,
saying children were hardly into sports these days, so
she should consider herself fortunate that her son was
a sports enthusiast. But the heat at the sporting ground
had started to trouble Nira. It was Javed who came up
with a solution. 'Madam, I have talked to our manager.
You can sit in his air-conditioned room.'

Nira was grateful for the offer. She started to carry
some of her books into the manager's room and enjoyed
the 'me time' that she got there. Javed would join her
occasionally, but would sit at a distance, conscious

they were by themselves in a closed enclosure. Nira encouraged him to talk. Javed would discuss the politics of Haryana and the country at large; sometimes, he talked about the lack of idealism in the youth. Nira who had initially perceived him as intellectually inferior was surprised at the depth of his knowledge. He was well read and came across as a sensitive and idealistic young man. What touched Nira was the deep respect he accorded her and his desire to learn from her.

One day, Javed greeted her with a box of sweets. 'My sister's marriage has been fixed. You must grace the occasion, Madam,' he said with a smile.

Nira was happy for him. She knew that he doted on his younger sister, but how could she go to his village? What would she tell Sameer? He would laugh at her and wonder about her sanity.

Just before Javed went on leave for the impending wedding, Nira tried to give him an envelope with some money in it. 'Shagun from my end. Please give it to your sister.'

Javed took the envelope, bowed his head in respect and put it back on the table. 'I can't accept it on her behalf. You give it to her whenever you meet her.'

Nira was deeply pained. She continued to reason with herself. It was impossible to attend a wedding like this. But her inner voice chided her for it. Javed's home was just a few kilometres away. The driver could have easily driven her there. Why did she not have the guts to ask Sameer? Also, once Javed was gone, she missed his presence at the cricket academy.

After Javed got back, Nira barely saw him. He was impersonal and distant on the rare occasions when they met. He was away for long stretches of time. Meanwhile, Tiya had started Grade 12 and a new set of tuitions were arranged for her. Nira was forced to accompany her as Sameer had strictly forbidden Tiya from going for her tuitions with only the driver for company. So, for almost a month, Nira did not go to the cricket academy. Tathya went by himself and seemed to be enjoying his new-found grown-up status.

One day, Tathya rushed to his mother with an envelope in his hand. 'Javed Sir asked me to give it to you. He is acting in a play and is inviting you!'

Nira was totally bewildered. Javed acting in a play? What on earth was Tathya talking about? The card was an invite to a theatre performance at Mandi House. Javed had also scrawled a tiny note in Hindi requesting her presence. Once again, Nira felt torn. As a teenager, she had loved theatre. She had been part of her college dramatics team and had also won a couple of prizes. But that was so long ago. She had not gone to Mandi House, the Delhi theatre-goer's Mecca, in decades. She now felt a strong urge to go for Javed's performance. She still remembered his hurt face when she had made excuses about her inability to attend his sister's wedding. She had lied well, but Javed had known the real reason, which is why he had politely declined her gift. Nira knew she needed to take her son into confidence.

'Don't breathe a word of this to Dad and Didi. We will tell them you have a late-evening practice session,' she whispered.

It turned out to be an evening Nira wouldn't forget in a lifetime. The performance was a rendition of Shakespeare's *Macbeth* in Hindi. Javed was scintillating as Banquo. The cast was young and their acting flawless. Time and again, Nira would squeeze Tathya's hands in sheer excitement. Tathya could not make much sense of the play, but he was happy for his mother's sake. Later, she went backstage to congratulate the cast. Javed excitedly introduced her to everyone. They were polite and warm. All of them were part of a local natya mandali. This was their first big production. Javed escorted her back to her car.

'I didn't know you were a theatre enthusiast,' Nira said.

'You never asked, Madam,' Javed answered quietly. 'But I know you love acting which is why I invited you.'

'You do? How?' It was Nira's turn to be surprised.

'You spoke of it often, Madam—about how much you enjoyed acting in college.'

***

Life has a way of seeping back into the humdrum, but Nira was finding it difficult to get back to her old contented self. Her mind constantly went back to those stolen moments at Mandi House. Mentally, she transformed into Lady Macbeth, a role which had won her great acclaim at the inter-college theatre competition in her undergraduate days. Surprisingly, she still remembered most of the dialogue. Sometimes, she spoke the lines out loud just to see if she still sounded the same.

'Madam, we are preparing for a new production. There is a role that is cut out for you. Would you like to audition?'

'Me, and audition for a play?' Nira stammered as Javed's voice on her mobile phone continued to tell her more about the play and why he thought she was suited for the role. That evening, Tathya brought home a packet with a bound script of the play, from the cricket academy. Nira snatched the packet and hid it among her clothes. No one should be privy to this new-found madness of hers. Luckily for her, Sameer was travelling on work. So, sneaking out in the evening for the audition was not as Herculean a task as she had imagined. She came back strangely elated. She had made it through the audition. It was a role after her own heart, but how on earth would she convince her family?

Day and night, an anxious Nira thought about it. She pictured a million ways in which she would break this news to Sameer. He would not be happy, but she would manage to convince him. She had successfully done so in the past. And it was just one performance. It wasn't as if she was taking up acting as a career. And she would ensure her children received as much attention as she was giving them now. She would not deprive them of her company. Sameer would understand. He had to. This was important for her.

Nira finally broke the news to Sameer. She spoke haltingly, much like a child who had scored poorly in her exams and had to face the daunting task of breaking the news to a hostile parent. She spoke of her meeting with Javed, his introducing her to the theatre group, her flawless performance at the audition, and the rehearsals that were to start shortly. She kept talking with her eyes glued to the floor. Once in a while, she would glance at Sameer who kept staring at his laptop. She assured him that her family wouldn't suffer if she went to the rehearsals and acted in the play. Sameer's jawline hardened and she knew he had been listening to her.

There was silence once she stopped speaking. Sameer continued to type with his eyes fixed on the laptop. Very quietly, with the nuanced voice of someone who thinks he is right, Sameer said, 'You can't go. It's most unbecoming of a Global Head's wife to be out on the streets acting with hooligans.'

'Sameer, Javed is a very nice person. You should meet him before you make up your mind.'

'Meet a cricket coach? I don't see any reason to meet him. And you don't need to see him either. I will arrange for Tathya to go for coaching elsewhere.'

He continued to type with his back to her. At least she was spared the indignity of shedding tears in front of him.

The next morning, things seemed like they were back to normal again. At the breakfast table, the children make the usual fuss over cereal. Sameer was laughing at Tiya's joke and he urged Nira to hurry up with his eggs. Sameer had two very important business meetings lined up. Nira played her part with great aplomb. She ran between the kitchen and the dining room, ensuring everyone was eating well, packing lunch boxes for the children, while simultaneously shouting out instructions to the maid. The milkman rang the bell. Their house buzzed with the sounds of the morning chaos.

After the children left for school and Sameer for his office, Nira sat down with her favourite cup of coffee. She stared long and hard at the cup as if willing it to help her find the right answer. Then, she picked up her mobile phone to make a call.

Late in the evening, as Nira stepped into the house, the morning's warmth had completely disappeared. Tathya ran up to her and hugged her. 'Where were you, Mom? We were so worried. Why was your phone switched off?'

Tiya was asking her the same question though her face reflected her father's annoyance.

Sameer stood ramrod straight, with his hands on his hips, anger writ large on his face.

'I had gone for the rehearsal of a play. Remember your Javed Sir had given me the script?' she addressed her son with a deliberate smile.

'I asked you not to,' Sameer spoke quietly, his anger seeping out through clenched teeth. 'I thought I had been quite clear about it.'

Nira extricated herself from her son's embrace and sat down on the sofa. Her children looked frightened. They had never seen their parents talking to each other like this.

'Tiya, take your brother and go to your room.' Sameer was still talking menacingly.

Quietly, but firmly, Nira said, 'They can remain here. There is nothing secretive about what I am doing that I need to hide it from them.'

In an even tone she talked to all of them about her role in the play. She also informed them that she would be gone every day, at this time 6 days a week.

Sameer had had enough. 'I had forbidden you from meeting that bunch of hooligans. Have you no shame? You are the mother of two grown-up children.' His cultured private school diction was slipping. 'This will very definitely not happen in my house.'

'This happens to be my house, not yours. And Sameer, I would really appreciate if you don't raise your voice,' Nira spoke in her newly acquired quiet tone. Every pore in her body was trembling with fear though she managed to appear calm. Nira the performer saw shock and disbelief slowly spreading across Sameer's face as he walked into the study, slamming the door shut behind him.

The next morning, as she sat down with her cup of coffee, a smile hovered on her lips when she started to mouth her dialogue. Her troubles were far from over, but for a change, she was battle-ready. The somnolent fire in her heart had been stoked and Nira happily basked in its glow.

4

Lipstick

I am a creeper in need of support to survive, but each time I curl around a tree, the gardener chops at its roots. So I am learning how to be a tree whose roots can't be hacked.

His mother walked into the room just as he was about to apply her new lipstick. She was startled. He was startled as well.

'What are you doing with my lipstick? she asked. 'It's new and I haven't used it so far. Couldn't you have waited a bit?'

He smiled and handed it back to her. 'I forgot to tell you, but I am playing Draupadi in our college production. Rehearsals start this evening.'

'Oh! Okay, take it then.' She smiled as she handed the lipstick back to him. Then she turned around and rushed to the kitchen as she had left the milk on the stove.

Vinay stared at the lipstick in silence and then lovingly applied it on his lips. He closed the door, drew the curtains and did a twirl in front of the mirror. His face lit up with an ethereal smile as he hugged himself.

Exactly half an hour later, he called out to his mother, 'Ma, I'm off.'

Dressed in a casual T-shirt and a pair of faded jeans, he gave his mother a big hug before leaving. As always, he was running late for class. His mother's gaze followed him as he crossed the narrow lane in front of their house and turned right to head to the bus stop.

Vinay was Malati's only child. Malati had lost her husband in a road accident. She remembered every detail of that fatal day when the family was returning from a wedding. Vinay was barely two years old. It was a hit-and-run case. Malati could remember hearing an ear-splitting sound before she fainted. Later, in the hospital, she would learn that a speeding car had rammed into their scooter. Fortunately, Malati and the child had escaped unhurt even though the doctors had failed to save her husband.

Malati's in-laws had been unforgiving. They had held her responsible for their son's death. Malati had walked out of her marital home to move to another city, with her young son in tow. She realised that from then on, she was going to be entirely on her own. She needed to fend for herself and her child.

She fought single-handedly to give Vinay a decent upbringing. It had been an uphill task. Her meagre salary was barely enough to tide over the mounting expenses. Yet, she did not give up, nor did Vinay let his mother down. A sensitive child, he tried to support her in his own way from a very young age. Reasonably good in studies, he had won several scholarships at school. This took care of his tuition fees. A good singer, he often performed in the religious functions held in his colony. Being the youngest member of a local bhajan mandali not only helped him earn money, but also built a lot of goodwill for the mother-son duo in the locality.

The neighbours had only good words for Malati and her son. They appreciated the fact that as a single mother, she had managed to achieve so much. They never ceased to be amazed at the closeness between the mother and the son. In an age when most children were self-obsessed, here was Vinay who was extremely solicitous of his mother's well-being. He helped her with domestic chores, ran errands, and most importantly, was polite and well behaved.

Malati's eyes brimmed with tears whenever she thought of her son. God had been kind to her. Not everyone had a son like hers. She was sure one day he would make a name for himself. Everyone in the neighbourhood said so and Malati liked to believe them. She knew God had put her through this long and arduous trial only to reward her in the end. Her son was going to make her proud.

Vinay was extremely close to his mother. She was all he had. He had no memories of his father, but this did not bother him at all. He was perfectly happy living with his mother; she meant the world to him. He knew he could do anything to make his mother happy, but of late, a few things had started to bother him. His secret was spilling over and he wasn't sure how long he would be able to keep it hidden from his mother.

From a very young age, Vinay had known he wasn't like boys his age. He didn't enjoy their rough and tough games nor did he like their boisterous talk. He cringed if a girl was being discussed or if one of his friends teased or harassed girls. Because of this, he spent long hours in the library or at home in the company of his mother. The neighbourhood boys branded him a sissy and shunned his company. Vinay's only release was his singing. He was truly gifted.

His social acceptance came from being part of the local band of singers who performed in all religious functions. The elders of the community saw this as something positive and were kind to the poor fatherless boy. However, Vinay started to retreat into his shell and over time, he realised he had no one to confide in. His sole friend and confidante was his mother, but there were things even a mother wouldn't understand.

It all started when the Khannas organised a
night-long Mata ki Chowki in their house. This was
a religious gathering where songs in praise of the
Goddess were sung to the beats of a dholak. Men
and women sang and danced away the night. Vinay
and his group of singers were invited to perform. Mr.
Khanna hadn't been one to cut back on the expenses.
An elaborate pandal had been built and the entire
neighbourhood was invited to take part in the
gathering which would be followed by a communal
dinner. Malati and Vinay were both looking forward
to it. Malati was happy as she would be spared from
cooking a meal and Vinay was thrilled he would earn
handsomely from this event.

An elaborate stage had been built and the lead
singer in Vinay's group started to sing. The crowd
participated by clapping and dancing to the beats.
Soon, the performers started to dance along with the
crowd. Vinay was transported as the music relaxed him
and his feet began to tap rhythmically. He draped a
chunni around his head and started to dance.

'Is he a boy or a girl?' Someone shouted from the
crowd. Malati noticed that all eyes were trained on her
son. Vinay was dancing, oblivious to everything. His
steps were fluid, graceful and lady-like as he moved
in circles with the chunni draped around his face like

a bride. Some people were laughing derisively now. Malati couldn't take it anymore and rushed back home.

Something had shattered. The rift between them continued to grow. For months, mother and son had not been able to speak to each other. They were forced to vacate their house and move to a different locality. People had started to make fun of Vinay openly. Some called him a eunuch, others suggested treatment. The verdict was unanimous: he was an aberration and therefore not fit to live in society unless he mended his ways.

In the initial days, Malati had tried to talk Vinay out of it. 'Try to behave like a man. Have more male friends,' she would say.

Vinay tried to reason with her, but to no avail. Over time, his mannerisms become more and more feminine. He even found male clothing abhorrent, but continued to wear them just to make his mother happy.

Their house, which used to smell of freshly cooked food and echo with mother-son banter fell silent. Malati still went to work as it was their sole means of sustenance. Vinay locked himself up in his room most of the time. Malati's health started to suffer. She had held on for all these years and worked like one possessed as she had big hopes from her son. Now, she almost dragged herself to work. Her body seemed to have shrunk and she started looking much older than her years.

Vinay's heart broke. What had he done to Ma—
she was now a ghost of her former self. Tears seared
his face as he watched his mother leave for work
every day.

One day, when Malati returned home, Vinay was
nowhere to be found. He had left a note behind saying
he was going away for good as he had become an
embarrassment for her. Malati was crazed with grief.
She sat in his room and howled in pain. It was as if a
part of her had been wrenched from her. For days,
she remained there, hugging his things and begging
the inanimate objects to bring Vinay back to her. She
called out his name, beseeching him to come back.
Her grief and guilt congealed into a solid mass which
grew heavier by the minute. Malati was on the verge of
losing her mind.

It was her job at the library that saved her. Her
colleagues were supportive; they even spoke on her
behalf to the owners to allow her to live in the room
adjoining the library premises. It was a public library
run by a Trust. Malati's job was to sit at the entrance
and check people's bags before they exited the library.
The salary was very low, but she had managed to
run her household with this money for so many
years. Moreover, the trustees were kind to her and
appreciated her dedication and honesty. The most

important reason for her holding on to this job was her belief that someday, her son might come looking for her and she needed to be there for him. However, as time passed, her hopes dimmed. Soon, there was nothing to look forward to. Life was a dark labyrinth of torturous memories from which there was no escape.

***

The first memory of Joy Malati had was her infectious smile. Most people looked dour when their bags were being checked. Some blinked as the sunlight startled them after stepping out of the closed confines of the library. Others yawned and some others looked bored. Joy had a huge backpack and as Malati rummaged through it, Joy smiled. Malati found herself smiling back. Soon, this became a routine. Joy was studying for a Ph.D. and she visited the library every day. She sat among the tomes lost to the world for hours. For lunch, she sat in the front lawns, laughing and joking with everyone. Malati found herself waiting for Joy's visit. There was something special about this girl and Malati was slowly succumbing to her charms.

Joy worked late into the evenings and Malati found herself wondering whether her family was worried about her. Her mother must be a lazy woman. What kind of mother would let her daughter walk around in the same set of clothes day after day? Also, the girl desperately needed feeding. She was thin to the point of being emaciated; her collar bones were sharp and on display as was her navel which peeped out of her undersized shirt. The girl was rugged and unkempt, but there was something nice about her. Malati waited for her to come to the library and greet her with a pleasant, 'Hello Aunty, how are you today?' before getting lost in her books or computer.

'Do you eat properly?' the words tumbled out before Malati could stop herself. She was checking Joy's bag as she was about to leave for the day. 'Sorry I didn't mean to...' Malati started to apologise, but Joy didn't seem offended.

'I love homemade food,' Joy smiled. 'You could treat me to a good meal anytime.'

'I...would love to. It's just that I live alone and I haven't cooked much in a while.'

'Any meal would be better than what they serve in the hostel. Can I come right away, Aunty? I'm ravenous.'

Malati was at a loss, but it was difficult to say no to this girl. With great reluctance, she took her to her quarters. Malati was extremely self-conscious as she led Joy to her room. This was the first time someone was visiting her here. It was cramped and messy as

Malati hardly bothered with housekeeping anymore. Vinay had robbed her of her will to live. Now she survived from one day to the next.

If Joy thought Malati was messy and unkempt, she didn't say so. She seemed to make herself at home. Perhaps the waif-like girl didn't need much space.

Malati fried perfectly round pooris and served them hot.

'You are an amazing cook, Aunty,' Joy squealed between mouthfuls. She ate with a healthy appetite and praised Malati's culinary skills to the skies.

Later, the two women chatted over steaming cups of ginger-laced tea.

Joy's real name was Jayita which meant 'winner'. She had won a fellowship for a research project which had brought her to this town. She lived in a working women's hostel quite close to the library. Her parents were bankers with transferable jobs and they lived in two different cities at the moment.

'Your mother allowed you to come to this big city all by yourself?' Malati couldn't help asking.

Joy burst out laughing. 'Aunty, it is my life. Why on earth would my parents stop me?'

Joy was bright, upright and opinionated— everything that Malati had been told a girl shouldn't be. Yet, she couldn't help but like her. It was so easy to be around Joy.

'Aunty, let's talk about you now. Have you lived here all your life?' Joy probed gently.

It took Malati a lot of time to open up. Unlike Joy, she was not used to talking about herself. Slowly, in bits and pieces, Malati started.

'There isn't very much to tell really. You will find my story very boring. I'm a poor uneducated woman. I don't know much...'

'That's for me to decide, Aunty.' Joy seemed wise beyond her years.

Malati broke down while talking about Vinay. It was her deepest secret, her badge of infamy—the reason why she now lived in complete isolation. She hated herself for having let him down. He was her only child, her darling boy whom she loved with every aching beat of a mother's heart.

'Aunty, there are many people like Vinay. You have no reason to be ashamed of him.' Joy's voice was calm and reassuring.

Malati had not forgotten the scorn and abuse her neighbours had heaped upon her. She had trouble believing Joy.

The next few months were a period of self-discovery for Malati. Joy read out books to her, made her watch films on her computer. She took her to self-help groups and introduced her to all kinds of people. She even introduced her to other parents who had treated their children exactly the way Malati had treated Vinay. Initially shy and hesitant, Malati slowly started to open up. An audacious thought had started to take shape in her mind—she might be able to find Vinay. Maybe all was not lost yet.

But first things first—she would have to dress properly—the way Vinay remembered her. Her house would have to be clean. Vinay had never seen her looking shoddy and unkempt. He would not bear to see her like that now. The spring in Malati's steps and the gleam in her eyes returned. She would definitely find her son. She would do all it took to find him. When he was back with her, she was going to do everything in her power to make him happy. She would make up for lost time.

For the first time in her life, Malati did not feel scared of what people might say about her or Vinay. Joy had given her the confidence to believe in herself. She was a strong woman, not a helpless victim. Vinay was *her* child and she would fight with every ounce of her strength to protect him. She would accept him the way he was. She would not let him down ever again.

Malati was a new woman. She had finally dared to come out of the closet.

5

Thammi

Ever since I can remember, Thammi and Ma had been at loggerheads. Not being able to take out her anger on Thammi, Ma would vent it on me. This was because Thammi, my paternal grandmother, and I had been the best of friends. 'Thammi' was my special name for her. She lived in a sprawling bungalow in Rasoolpur, on the outskirts of Kolkata, with her attendant, Joba Pishi, a small bird-like woman who oversaw the running of the household, did the shopping and cooked delicious meals. My father addressed her as Didi or elder sister so, naturally she became my Pishi. I was told Joba Pishi was Thammi's right-hand woman and was not to be mistaken for a servant. I was too young to register these differences or to care one way or the other.

My grandfather had passed away when I was very young. My only memories of him are from the various photographs in Thammi's room. My favourite is a family photograph in which both Ma and Thammi are smiling at the camera and I am at the centre, seated on Thakurda's lap. Even Joba Pishi is in the photograph, cradling her daughter Lalita in her arms. This was my world through the magical phase of life called childhood.

Thammi's house was everything our house in Kolkata was not. It boasted of large rooms with high ceilings and a huge garden which seemed to have a life of its own. Apart from a few flowering plants was a profusion of trees and birds who had built their nests there. To my young mind, this was a jungle, and Lalita and I would try to jump from one branch to the other, pretending to be Mowgli and Baloo.

Lalita was agile and managed to negotiate the 'jungle' much better than me. I fell down and managed to injure myself a few times. Thammi would smile and say, 'It's part of growing up. Next time, just be more careful.' Ma would throw a fit and threaten Baba that she would never send me to Thammi's place again. This impasse would hold till the next summer vacations when Baba would gear up to visit his mother again. I would fuss and cry so much that he would be forced to take me along and then my mother would relent and join us. Through our month-long stay there, Ma would be sullen, unfriendly and unreasonably irritable while I would have a whale of a time.

I never understood what irritated Ma more—Joba Pishi's cooking and Baba's high praise for it, or Thammi and Baba's 'secret' talks in Thakurda's library, or Thammi's leniency with me. I was not required to follow any particular schedule during my stay with her. She allowed me to run wild with Lalita and her friends. We were a boisterous lot running down the streets, invading gardens, plucking fruits and jumping over puddles. When Lalita and I came back home, we tiptoed in through the back entrance. Joba Pishi would nod her head in disapproval, but quickly take charge of me lest Ma caught a glimpse of me. She would bathe me and clean me up, but even then, Ma would find something wrong with me. At night, when I would fall asleep from sheer exhaustion, I would feel Ma's fingers running through my hair. She was convinced I had lice due to my proximity with Lalita.

When it was time to return, I would cry all the way back to Kolkata. Ma would start cheering up the minute our car hit the highway. My misery and Ma's merriment seemed almost inversely proportionate. Back home, she would be her usual happy self. I would be subjected to two rounds of body and hair scrubbing till she was satisfied I wasn't carrying any germs from my stay in Thammi's house. School would start and everything would get back to 'normal'. In my head, I would keep counting the days for my next visit to Thammi's.

***

It had been almost two years since I had visited Thammi. My school-leaving exams, tuitions and piano classes had ensured I was constructively occupied from dawn to dusk. Now I also had close friends with whom I hung around in malls and movie theatres. I thought of Thammi often, but I no longer missed her with my former intensity. Thammi seemed to sense this and over time, her calls on my mobile phone decreased in frequency. I didn't bother myself with it. Ma seemed really happy with this new turn of events.

I had my first 'adult' conversation with Ma when I was about to begin college in a new city far away from home. She was worried and fidgety, packing and repacking my things while advising me on how to make the most of college life. Finally, when she realised she could not pack anything else into my suitcase, she let go of it reluctantly. Then the two of us sat down to sip tea companionably on our verandah.

'Ma, why do you hate Thammi so much?' I asked.

Her hand shook and she spilt some tea. She stared hard into her cup almost as if the answer to my question lay there.

'I don't hate her. I think I just don't like her,' she muttered.

'Why?'

'She is a peculiar woman. She loves Gita as much as her own son—your father. She treats you at par with Lalita and all her students. Isn't that strange? You are her only grandchild. Has she ever made you feel special?'

Ma made me think of things I had never worried about before. Sure, Thammi wasn't like any other grandmother I knew. She preferred to live on her own and though she had only one biological son—my father—she was a mother to many in that village. Men and women came to her with their problems. She advised them and did everything in her power to help them. She ran an NGO to help the needy and the destitute, and everyone in the village respected her. And yes, Ma was right, Thammi never made my father or me feel special in any way. We were like everyone else. I can't say why, but my heart hardened a little towards Thammi. I was going to begin a new life, but she hadn't even bothered to call me. Thammi was indeed a strange lady!

'Also, I'm a little jealous,' Ma continued in a subdued voice. 'I'm jealous of her independence. Look at how she continues to live on her own terms even today. It's not easy to be the wife of her only child. Your Baba dotes on her. His world begins and ends with his mother. And then there is my only daughter who also seemed to prefer her Thammi over me.'

'That's not true, Ma…' I held her hand. She brought it to her lips in a rare show of affection as she brushed off her tears with the other hand.

'Come on, time for your dinner. Remember to eat your meals on time. I don't want any complaints from your hostel warden. She appears to be a strict lady.'

Our time for confidences was over. She was my Ma again—bossy, irritating and opinionated. I obeyed her in silence. My heart was beating very fast. It would be the start of a new life for me from tomorrow, away from the familiar. I was excited, but also a little scared.

The first few months, I missed home and was constantly in touch with everyone, but slowly, college life grew on me. The course work was demanding as were my friends and love interests. Calls home became few and far between. My new life carried me forward at breakneck speed and I allowed it to get the better of me. I enjoyed my new-found freedom and confidence. Undaunted by my reluctance to talk much, Ma still called to ask after me, but there was an ocean of silence between Thammi and me, made worse by her refusal to own a mobile phone and my complete disdain for letter writing. On the few occasions when we talked on her landline, the conversations were forced and bordered on exchanging inanities. Soon we stopped reaching out to each other. I kept track of her well-being through Ma and Baba. I had moved on mentally, and the goings-on in and around Kolkata did not interest me much.

***

Early one morning, the mobile phone rang. I woke up with a start, wondering who could be calling me at this hour. Ma was on the line and tried to break the news as gently as possible. Thammi was unwell, she said, but I knew. I had ignored Thammi and she had found a way to get back at me. My Thammi was no more. It felt like an unbearable body blow.

I could never have imagined that my trip back home would be fraught with so much pain. The journey from the airport to her house and the grief of not finding her there couldn't be expressed in words. Baba, dressed in his mourning whites and his head shorn was a man I didn't recognise. Joba Pishi seemed to have shrunk even more and wasn't capable of saying or doing anything. The only person who seemed to be in control of things was Ma, who was ably assisted by

Lalita. Lalita had changed completely from the young girl I once knew. She was still her slim and agile self, but she was no longer my friend and co-conspirator. She wore a sari and all the symbols of a married woman and looked worn down. With her help, Ma could organise the funeral and take adequate care of the many visitors who came to express their condolences. I did not recognise this grown-up Lalita. Nor did I recognise Ma who seemed to have grown quite close to both Joba Pishi and Lalita. Ma assured Joba Pishi that she could stay at Thammi's house forever. While departing from the house, Ma held Joba Pishi in a tight embrace. It was as if all petty jealousies had been washed off in the wake of the huge tragedy that had befallen us.

I almost heaved a sigh of relief when I was back in my familiar two-room apartment in London, dealing with work pressure. Being immersed in work was the best way to get over the pain and guilt I felt over the way Thammi and I had drifted apart. Slowly and steadily, I started healing, but I knew it would be a long time before I could be whole again.

***

This time round, yet another early morning call startled me out of my sleep. It was Ma again who spoke with an urgency I had never heard in her voice before. 'Come as soon as possible. We have a major problem.' She would not divulge anything else over the phone, so I was forced to take leave from the law firm where I worked and head back to Kolkata.

Life is an exam with an unknown syllabus. That is the exact feeling I had when I met Lalita. My job had trained me to defend battered women, but I had never met one before. Also, the fact that we had had a shared childhood made things even more difficult for me.

Lalita had studied up to Grade 10 when Joba Pishi found a match for her. She had been married off against Thammi's wishes. Now, after three children and a decade of marriage, Lalita had finally dared to call it quits. She had come back to her mother, vowing to never go back to her husband again. I was called in to counsel her since I had trained as a lawyer. Baba had been totally against Ma sending for me. He had cited my work commitments and travel expenses, but Ma had insisted. Annoyed, he had refused to accompany her, so for the first time in her life, Ma was visiting Rasoolpur without him.

It felt strange to be at Thammi's house in her absence. We would have been a very sorry group if Lalita's daughters had not been there. They ran around in the garden and played games, reminding me of the time when Lalita and I were of that age. In the evening, after the children were tucked in, Ma, Joba Pishi, Lalita and I sat down to talk. Lalita told us her story.

The initial phase of her marriage had been reasonably good. Things had worsened after she gave birth to three daughters in a row. Her husband had developed a drinking problem and had turned abusive. In the beginning, Lalita put up with it to keep the marriage going, but soon things started to spiral out of control. The forced back-to-back pregnancies and the abuse that followed the birth of the girls had started to take a toll on Lalita. She was mentally and physically broken. Alarmed by her daughter's rapidly deteriorating condition, Joba Pishi had informed Ma, who had gone to Lalita's house all alone. She had been threatened by Lalita's husband, but Ma had remained unfazed. She had managed to walk out with Lalita and the children.

'Your mother saved my daughter,' Joba Pishi told me, sniffing into her sari border.

I stared at Ma. I had always thought her to be rather conservative and an oddly reserved woman. I could have believed my Thammi doing something like this, but not Ma.

She smiled a sad smile. 'Always that comparison with your Thammi. Your father did it all the time and now even you...and I invariably fall short, don't I?'

I squeezed her hand tightly. 'No, Ma, you are as brave as Thammi. No one could have handled this like you did. You took such good care of Joba Pishi after Thammi's death and what you have done for Lalita is beyond words... Wish Thammi was alive to see all this.'

As if on cue, all of us turned towards Thammi's portrait. She seemed to be smiling back at us.

I called my office in London and applied for long leave. I would stay here with Joba Pishi, Lalita and the girls and fight Lalita's case. I would ensure that the girls got their due. Suddenly, after years, I felt lighter. Maybe this would be my way of making it up to Thammi; I had never been able to forgive myself for having treated her the way I did during my early years in college.

***

It has been seven long years. I have not been able to go back. There is so much to do here. Ma has taken charge of Thammi's NGO. She runs it just as smoothly and the villagers accord her the same respect they used to give Thammi. Together, we are bringing up Lalita's daughters. Lalita wants them to become like me. Joba Pishi still cooks the world's best food, but Ma doesn't get upset when Baba praises her culinary skills these days. She laughs and thanks Joba Pishi for sparing her the drudgery of the kitchen.

Our lives seemed to have fallen into a strange pattern. While fighting Lalita's case, I came across several other women who needed legal assistance. There were others who needed counselling. My hands were always full—I worked from morning till late at night, but felt satisfied. It was as if I wasn't running away anymore.

Ma seamlessly taking over from where Thammi had left off was yet another life lesson for me. We realised Thammi had left us all with tasks she hadn't forced upon any of us. Perhaps in her uncanny way, she had always known what all of us took so long to realise—there was something much larger than self-gratification. Thammi had shown us how to live our lives, how it was imperative to build upon the edifice she had constructed. At last, Ma and I had managed to make peace with Thammi.

6

Laila

She opened her bleary eyes when the cat, all seven pounds of squirming flesh, was up on her belly. Squinting at the sunlight streaming in from the open window, she discovered she was now the weary possessor of a pounding headache and at some point, had also managed to lose both a tooth and a spouse. Laila blinked and half-raised herself to draw the curtains. Her head was heavy and she needed a few more hours before she could face the world. She knew her marriage was definitely over.

She managed to open her eyes again and noticed that some solicitous soul had left a glass of water on her bedstead. Was it Meera the maid who had come to her rescue again? The Lord be praised! It was chilled lemonade and that made her head clear up a bit. She gulped the drink greedily as she firmly pushed Kitty away. Kitty settled down on the spot where she had been pushed to, and continued to sleep. For the umpteenth time, Laila wished she could exchange places with Kitty. They were an odd couple—one wildly happy and satiated, the other, terribly sad.

Laila forced herself to get up. She looked around and the usual mess met her eyes—clothes, books, CDs where they shouldn't be. The clothes were mostly hers, she realised, with a pang of guilt, but the books and CDs were his. Who in these digital times read books and listened to CDs? Arun did, and what was worse was that she had fallen for him because he had appeared so different. He was well read, articulate, laid back and an intellectual, and it was because of him she was in this mess. A voice inside her head was contradicting her and speaking in her sister's voice, 'You are stewing in a self-created mess, Laila. Wake up and take stock of your life.'

'Mona?' Laila wanted to reach out, but as always, her sister wasn't there. She was never around when she needed her. She surfaced to reprimand her only sister and then disappeared almost instantly. Mona was always busy and never had a kind word for Laila. The whole world is conspiring against me, Laila thought as she made a Herculean effort to sit up. She felt her headache ebbing slowly. She could hear Mona speaking inside her head again. 'Sort out your life, girl. No one else will do it for you.'

Laila started to pick up the clothes from the floor and fold them into neat piles, which would eventually go into the cupboard. She had pulled them out to get dressed for the Saturday night party. She had thoroughly enjoyed herself though she wasn't really the partying type, but the emptiness in the house had been getting to her. Why on earth were Arun's books and CDs strewn all over the place? She tried to cast her mind back, but could barely remember a thing. Well, one thing was for sure—she had ruined the party and her co-workers weren't going to invite her again anytime soon. She wondered whether she still had her job. Did a drunken brawl deserve disciplinary action? Laila had no idea; she wasn't capable of thinking straight yet.

So, how had she landed in this mess? It was simple— she had the knack of moving from one disaster to the next. It all started when she agreed to marry Arun. No, actually, it had started even earlier. Her life had been a perpetual mess because of Mona. God knows what she had done to deserve Mona. Mona was tall, beautiful, purposeful and successful—everything Laila was not. Mona had further messed up her life by naming her after her favourite Bollywood number. Laila didn't know what she hated more—Mona's bossy attitude or the silly name she was stuck with. For the time being, she was forced to live with both and suffer.

Laila could barely remember her parents. They had passed away in an accident. She had been brought up entirely by Mona who was a parent and sister rolled into one. Time and again, she had tried to break out of Mona's colossal shadow, but that was not to be. Marriage to Arun was a desperate escape bid, but that too had crashed, leaving her bruised. Ever since Laila could remember, it had just been the two of them, or rather, it was just her since Mona was always busy.

Laila never had a house. Mona worked at a hotel and she had been allotted a room in the hotel premises. From the time Laila could remember, that room had been their home. There was barely space for two in there, but Mona said this arrangement worked best for her and the hotel. It provided her security and there was no travelling involved. And if it worked well for Mona, Laila had little choice but to adjust.

Laila hated their cramped room. When she visited friends from school, she would be mesmerised by their houses, which had more rooms than the number of people who lived there. There was a dedicated space for sitting, eating and cooking. It seemed so inviting and cozy. Nobody lived in a 'room' even if the room happened to be in a five-star hotel.

When Laila was young, she used to have friends. The little girls and boys loved the hotel and thought she was privileged to be living there. The exotic food never ceased to amaze them. Mona was a super-hit with them. She jumped on the sofa with the children and allowed them to eat on the bed. She wasn't like the other grown-ups who liked to discipline the kids. However, this stopped when Laila hit her teens. She noticed the boys in her class flirted outrageously with Mona who reciprocated playfully. The circle of gossip grew and Laila started to distance herself from her friends. Soon, she was a loner who had no one but Mona to fall back on. And if Mona noticed any of this, she never discussed it with her.

Mona prospered in her job—she loved the hotel and the hotel loved her back. Her employers doted on her. The only person who felt left out and couldn't fit in anywhere was Laila. She shrank further into herself, became a certified loner and took refuge in her books.

The only constant in Laila's life in school, college and Business School was the rapid increase in the thickness of her glasses and her waistline. She learnt to take offensive jokes in her stride. It reached a point when she wondered whether her second name was 'fatso', 'walrus' or 'moti chashmish'. She learnt to smile when someone kinder told her, 'But round is also a shape!' Her academic excellence helped her land a job with a leading multinational. Life seemed to take a turn for the better, and then she met Arun.

Arun was everything Laila was not. Well spoken, well read and suave, he had a mind of his own. He was the first man Laila had met who showed more interest in her than in her sister. In fact, he was the only man she knew who wasn't charmed by Mona. He was polite and deferential to her, not flirtatious and over friendly. He had a beautiful flat overlooking the hills, and for the first time, Laila felt herself breathing fresh air when she stepped out on to his balcony. More than the scenic beauty, it was the thought that there would be space to move around, entertain friends and freedom to escape Mona's chaotic lifestyle that drew her close to Arun.

Their courtship was brief—a few rounds of coffee at the office canteen and coffee shops, a couple of drinks on his terrace and a spate of passionate lovemaking decided things in Arun's favour. Laila decided that she loved him deeply and wanted him to be hers for a lifetime. Mona had asked her to take things easy, but Laila refused to listen to her. This act of rebellion came as a shock to both the sisters. Mona was hurt and kept her distance from the couple.

Laila, heady with the success of her rebellion, chose to concentrate on her new life. The roller-coaster affair ended in a court marriage, and Laila finally moved out of the claustrophobic room into a house of her own. She wasn't sure what she loved more—Arun or the beautiful flat with balconies overlooking the hills.

Life with Arun was simple with no trace of excess. He was still paying off his EMIs on the car and the house. With Laila, he had an easy friendship and he tried to introduce her to his world of music and books. He was happy tinkering with pots and pans in the kitchen while humming a Tagore song. In the first year of marriage, Laila was mesmerised with Arun's way of life. He was relaxed and content, unlike Mona who always seemed to rush through life. He wasn't particularly ambitious and could lose himself in Tagore's words or Sufi music. Laila tried to learn and adapt and the two of them were happy together. After the initial headiness of love had worn off, Laila tried to reach out to Mona, but Mona continued to remain distant. It broke Laila's heart, but she would never allow Mona to find out how much she missed her.

Boredom crept into the marriage even before Laila was aware of it. What had seemed endearing earlier started to irritate her. Laila couldn't understand how Arun could be completely careless about bills that needed to be paid or how he would manage to wear a wrinkled shirt to a meeting. He would read a book while drinking his morning tea and be completely oblivious to what Laila was saying. He would forget to dry the bathroom floor. His wet towel would be on the bed rather than on the clothesline. Soon, Laila was convinced Arun was an overgrown baby on the lookout for a mother rather than a companion.

Her pent-up irritation started to break out into full-blown wars. Arun chose to come home late from work and would get out of the house as early as possible. Laila went back to her chaotic over-eating, drawing solace from pastries and sugary cups of tea. She was depressive and angry, and tried to reach out to Mona yet again, but Mona was in Australia and did not take her calls. Laila's life slipped into a familiar trajectory of boredom and loneliness as she realised with a shock that she was left with only Kitty for company.

It was a Saturday morning of a pleasant summer weekend and the flowers on Laila's terrace garden were in full bloom, but she hardly noticed them. She tried to drown her sorrow in two tall glasses of iced tea made to perfection by Meera, her part-time help. Laila was fond of Meera because she plied Laila with food whenever she was feeling low. She was completely non-judgemental and Laila liked to believe her confidences were safe with her. She poured her heart out to Meera who came up with ready solutions. She prescribed a clove paste for Laila's aching tooth and an evening out with friends to get her out of her present state. Meera's clove paste proved to be a miracle cure and Laila was persuaded into believing that an evening out might actually do her some good.

The HR team in her office was meeting over cocktails in the evening. Laila had made her excuse citing the toothache, but on an impulse she agreed to go. Arun was out of town for a week on work. Laila was confused about her feelings for him. She missed him, but mostly she was upset with him and sought an unconditional apology for his behaviour. Arun behaved like nothing had changed between them and carried on with his life—a trait Laila loathed.

She dressed with care for the party. Meera helped her choose her clothes—a black knee-length dress with a tantalisingly deep neckline. Black made her look somewhat slimmer. She set it off with a diamond choker and looked at herself in the mirror for a long time without stirring. She looked beautiful and suddenly realised she missed Arun. How he would have loved to see her like this! The party would be the last thing on his mind, she thought, smiling mischievously to herself.

***

She hit the floor with a vengeance. She had wowed to dance away her sorrows and she did exactly that. The drinks helped. Soon, she was getting bolder and attracting more attention than she would have normally desired. But what the heck, she was enjoying it! Everything was going great till her eyes fell on him. He was dancing with someone—two bodies entwined as they swayed as one to the music. The girl had her hand around his neck and her fingers were playing with his hair.

With a shock, Laila realised it was Arun and her colleague Zeenat. Zeenat seemed to be whispering something in Arun's ear as he playfully pulled her closer to him. Arun had lied to her—he hadn't gone out of town. He had known Laila wouldn't attend the party, so he chose to make a spectacle of himself with this woman. The audacity of the act shook Laila to the core. She was trembling with rage when she attacked the unsuspecting duo. Arun took a step back and Laila hit Zeenat with all her strength. An obviously startled Zeenat hit back in self-defence. Laila fell to the floor with a thud as her jaw caught the end of the table. She could taste blood before passing out.

It was Sunday afternoon by the time Laila's head started to clear up. There was a cut on her jaw. The offending tooth had fallen off, but luckily that was all. Miraculously, she was safe in her apartment and things appeared to be under control. And then it all came back to her. Arun was with another woman. She had lost him for good. She felt herself drowning in a fit of rage and sorrow as she burst into tears. She sobbed uncontrollably, calling out to him. She knew it was over and Arun was not the kind of man who believed in making compromises in relationships. She registered with a shock that she loved him. She loved him in spite of his strange ways. She liked having him around. Without him, she felt incomplete. Arun could be infuriating at times, but she couldn't imagine living without him.

And then, as if by magic, Arun was by her side. He was holding her and kissing her like he would never let her go. Laila pushed him back.

'How dare you, Arun! How dare you cheat on me?' she could hear herself screaming.

But Arun was not fighting back. He was smiling as he held the rebellious Laila close to him.

'Gosh, Laila what an absolute moron you are.' Mona seemed to have appeared out of nowhere and she stood around giving Laila the 'look'. 'Laila, you haven't guessed yet.' Mona was her usual self—elder sisterly and infuriating.

'Mona?' Laila was caught off guard. This had to be a dream. She lay back on the bed and closed her eyes.

Then, she opened her eyes just enough to see Mona standing right there. Mona and Arun exchanged a conspiratorial look and smile.

Despite her sorry state, Laila was indignant. She sat up and glared at them.

'Laila, haven't you guessed yet? Arun and I hatched a plan to knock some sense into you and we got Malini and Zeenat to help us. But you crazy woman—you actually hit Zeenat! I have no idea how I'll pacify her. You have never behaved this way before.' Mona pulled a wry face. She was her usual self—the bossy elder sister.

Suddenly, the world seemed right. Kitty saw this as a perfect opportunity to climb back on to her stomach and snooze off. This time, Laila let her be. She felt happy in the presence of the two people she loved the most. She knew this was a fleeting moment and tomorrow she might not feel the same. But tomorrow was another day and she would face it, chin up. Today was what mattered. Laila smiled. She could hear Kitty purring happily curled up on her tummy.

7

The Second Wife

The procession wound its way through the narrow lanes of Kolkata as the sounds of 'Vande Mataram' rent the air. A woman quietly stepped onto the terrace. She stood at the railing to take in the sight. From her aristocratic bearing, she looked every bit the mistress of the house. But her actions were guarded and she took every precaution to not be seen. The sari's aanchal was pulled forward and veiled her face from the world. As she stared at the procession, her eyes welled up with unshed tears. Unbeknownst to her, her aanchal slipped back, revealing her incredibly beautiful face. She hastened to cover her face again. Then slowly she walked across the terrace, went down the stairs and slipped out of the house.

***

Kusumbala's daughters were named after flowers–Champa and Bela. Champa Rani was as fair as the eponymous champa phool, with a face that resembled Goddess Durga's. Bela was darker than her sister, and her chiselled face shone with a unique glow. Her hair cascaded down to her waist. The firmness of her body and her dark evocative eyes bestowed a touch of sensuality on her.

Champa was always the quieter one. She would sit in a corner playing with her earthen dolls. Bela had no time for such things. Instead, she would roam the village climbing trees, plucking fruit and fishing in the pond. She was the undisputed leader of a gang of boys who treated her like one of their own. Together they raided every fruit-laden tree and stealthily fished in the neighbourhood ponds. Every single day, someone or the other would turn up at home to complain about Bela and her waywardness. 'Who on earth would marry a girl like this?' the neighbourhood women grumbled.

After Champa's birth, Kusum lost two precious male children during childbirth. When Bela was born, Kusum was sure she too would follow her brothers in death, so she chose to be indifferent to the infant. But Bela was determined to live. She cried lustily till her mother was forced to feed her.

When Bela was barely three months old, tragedy struck—her father suddenly died of a heart attack. While Kusum was widowed at a very young age, the elders in the family pinned the blame on Bela calling her inauspicious. First, she had 'eaten' her brothers, and now, her father.

Unaware of the evil deeds she had supposedly committed, Bela continued to grow like a bamboo reed watered by the rains. Everything about her was earthy and solid. She was exceptionally good in studies as well, But of what use would that be to her, wondered Kusum. Soon Bela would be pulled out of the pathshala and married off.

Though Kusum never admitted it, she loved Bela deeply. She was certain her younger daughter had been cut out for bigger things in life. 'O, why did God make her a woman? A woman's life begins and ends in the kitchen.' At the thought, a tear would roll down her eyes unbidden. Yet, the next morning, she would complain loudly to her gods for having cursed her with this changeling of a child.

Champa's beauty was the talk of Kolkata and Kusum was flooded with marriage proposals for her elder daughter. The decision however wasn't hers to make. Champa's uncles fixed the marriage and soon the twelve-year-old bid a teary goodbye to all her childhood moorings and became the daughter-in-law of the Dutta household of Kolkata. At one point of time, the Duttas had been a well-to-do family. Now, what remained was a sprawling ungainly mansion in desperate need of repairs, and a good name in the society which was deemed even more important than preserving their dwindling fortunes.

Clad in a red banarasi sari and a veil during the ceremony, Champa had barely had a glimpse of her husband. She met him much later at their phoolsajja when the young bride sat on a flower-bedecked bed as her husband joined her. He was tall—taller than any man she had ever seen. Champa's heart went cold with an unknown fear.

Ratan was a strapping youth of twenty who worked as a landowner's scribe. His passion was football. Like Champa, he too was confused about what he was required to do with this new addition in his life. He understood he had to be dominating because his friends had warned him against being kind to women. 'It's a game of one-upmanship. Right from the outset, you must show her who's the boss,' they had insisted. At home, Ratan had learnt no better.

Without saying much to his bride, he lay on the bed, stretched out his legs and asked her to press them. Later that night, he woke up to find her fast asleep with her head on his feet. His slight movement woke her up and she started pressing his legs again. Ratan drifted back to sleep, a contended man—this girl would do his bidding without asking questions. He did not have much experience with women but her servility pleased him no end.

Over the next five years, they became parents to two girls. With every birth, an increasingly enraged Ratan heaped curses on Champa for her inability to give him a male heir. After each childbirth, Champa grew thinner and weaker till, finally, at the tender age of seventeen, she breathed her last.

Meanwhile, Bela outgrew her frocks and started to wear saris. On reaching puberty, she was forced to discontinue school. No longer did she have a free run of the neighbourhood with the boys. Now she found solace in the books that she read. Kusum knew it was inauspicious for a girl to read, but she was loath to deny her daughter these little pleasures, knowing the tough times that would follow once she got married. Both Kusum and Bela had longed to see Champa, but the Dutta household being patriarchal to the hilt, Champa had rarely been allowed to visit her parental home.

And then came the shocking news of Champa's death. Kusum and Bela were devastated. Soon word was out that Ratan was looking for another bride. And one day, Ratan came visiting with his daughters. He convinced Kusum that by marrying Bela, he would be doing right by his daughters. Bela being their aunt would love them as her own and would never behave like the proverbial stepmother. Bela's uncles were overjoyed at the idea—they would not have to spend much on this wedding.

Kusum shed bitter tears, but there was little she could do to prevent the marriage. So, she steeled herself and watched her little girl being adorned in a red banarasi sari and whisked off to the Dutta household as Ratan's second wife.

Before leaving home, Bela had touched her books one last time and sobbed inconsolably. Later, a dry-eyed Bela had touched her mother's feet to seek her blessings, and said her final goodbye. That was enough to get her in-laws' tongues wagging—which girl left her home without howling? Heaven knew they were taking home with them a daini.

The name stuck. In the Dutta household, Bela was indeed a daini. She had bewitched Ratan. It was already a year since the marriage, but Ratan's eyes followed her everywhere. Bela did not give Ratan the much-desired male child. In fact, she did not conceive at all. Despite the passage of time, she remained her tall, stately self. The only change in her was the bright red vermilion she wore in the parting of her hair. She took excellent care of her nieces and even her worst enemy could not find fault with her devotion towards them. Yet, Kusum was worried. Bela seemed to have changed. She had completely withdrawn into herself. She performed her duties like an automaton. Only the fire in her eyes would be reminiscent of her erstwhile self, but she took care to keep her gaze down, and her face remained firmly covered with her sari's aanchal. There was no knowing what was on her mind.

Years went by. Bela fulfilled her duty of being the perfect mother. The girls were married off into prosperous Kolkata households. Bela still looked the same. Only now she had taken to wearing white saris. After all, she had become a mother-in-law. Ratan tried to protest. 'You're not even their real mother.'

Bela smiled, 'Didi would've done the same. It's either her or me. How does it matter?'

Ratan disliked Champa's name being mentioned in the house. She was someone he had never cared for. But Bela was different. She had won his heart completely. He tried hard to please her, but the more he tried, the further she seemed to drift away. He even went against his mother's diktat and started to buy her books. She devoured them hungrily, but would never ask him to get anything for her. How he longed for her to ask him for something…anything. Even the jewellery he had gifted her, she had passed on to her nieces as dowry. Her sari was crisp cotton, white in colour with the mandatory red border. Apart from a thin neck-piece and a pair of bangles, she wore no jewellery. Looking at her, one would think she was undergoing severe penance. She performed her duty towards everyone, but continued to remain aloof and distant. So much so that Ratan started growing wary of her ways. He loved her to distraction. She never thwarted his advances nor did she crave for them. She was indifferent to all his ministrations.

Over time, Ratan changed completely. Gone were his arrogance and brusqueness. His appearance changed too. He was now a pot-bellied, balding, middle-aged man incurably in love with the still very beautiful Bela. The gossip in the neighbourhood was that Bela had deliberately not had a child as she wanted to maintain her figure. And it is with her maidenly body and her long lustrous locks that she continued to bewitch her husband.

'She has done some magic,' they whispered nodding their heads though inwardly they envied the attention her husband showered on her—a mere childless woman.

***

It was the time when the country was going through a major political upheaval. The freedom struggle was rapidly gaining ground. The Dutta household tried its best to insulate itself from the world outside, but it wasn't easy to hold this tide in check. Young men were seen marching on the streets of Kolkata brandishing banners and the cries of 'Vande Mataram' filled the neighbourhood

One day, a young boy turned up at the Dutta household, seeking alms for the struggle. Without a moment's hesitation, Bela took off every piece of ornament she had been wearing and handed them to him. He stared at her in surprise.

'These must be very expensive, Ma. Are you sure you want to part with all of them?'

'Yes, keep them.' Then for the first time in years, Bela's voice trembled with the force of her emotions. 'Aren't there any women in your group? Don't women participate in the struggle?'

'They do, Ma. Our leaders want women to lead from the front. They say a one-legged person can't win a race!"

Since that day, Ratan noticed a change in Bela. There was a feverish excitement about her. She devoured the newspapers hungrily, as if willing them to perform some miracle. She waited for him to return from work and wanted him to talk about the freedom movement. Ratan was bewildered. Unlike Bela, he wasn't touched by the struggle. For him, the struggle was ludicrous and a space for licentiousness. Whoever heard of women from respectable families taking to the streets to protest?

Bela's mother-in-law prophesied that the dreaded Kaliyug had arrived, and the world would soon come to an end. But Ratan tried to be patient with his beloved second wife. What if she lapsed back into her old withdrawn self? Why could she not be like the other women around him?

One day, when such a procession wound its way through the narrow lanes below the Dutta household, Bela quietly went up to the terrace for a better view. Yes, the boy had been right. There were women right in the front, holding banners and singing 'Vande Mataram'. Endless rivulets of tears streamed down Bela's cheeks. Then she slowly walked across the terrace, went down the stairs and slipped out of the house.

***

In the old houses leaning on each other along the narrow lanes of Kolkata, where Bela once lived in the Dutta household, her story is told even today—

she had brought shame upon her people and her community; she was a fallen woman; who would have thought a happily married woman from a respectable family would abandon the comforts of her husband's home to heed the call of such unbridled freedom from the world outside?

But in the confines of her room, the old and frail Kusum shed tears of joy. At last, her Bela was free.

8

Happy Times

The landline was ringing with its usual intensity—loud, urgent, disruptive. Who could be calling at this hour? Aisha reached for her glasses and felt around for her mobile phone. The screen came to life. It was 5.30 in the morning. Time to get up anyway. Aisha firmly ignored the phone and stepped into the bathroom. The phone rang again with an unusual urgency.

Aisha's contacts were few and she lived a disciplined life where every waking hour of her day was accounted for. Her morning began with yoga in the front lawn, followed by her tending to her plants and talking to the gardener. After a frugal breakfast, she would attend to her mails and do her typing on her laptop in her office room. She would have her lunch and continue to work till five in the evening. Late evenings would find her curled up on her favourite sofa, talking on the phone while the television droned on in the background.

A mandatory call to Kabir and Saima was made to assure them that she was doing fine. At eight, her maid Dona would summon her for dinner after which she would retreat to her bedroom and read till she fell asleep. Her routine would be tweaked a little if either Kabir or Saima was visiting or if she was going out with her friends. For years, Aisha had followed this routine and it had become a part of her.

The phone was ringing again—the sound seemed to have become louder. Aisha's 'hello' had irritation written all over it.

'Bibiji, kahan thi aap? Where were you?'

'Raj Singh?' She had not heard his voice for five long years. 'Raj Singh, is everything alright?' Aisha could sense the panic in his voice. Why was he calling her?

'No, Bibiji. Things are not alright. Please come here right now. Please.' Raj Singh was crying.

Something terrible must have had happened there, but why was Raj Singh calling her? Aisha quickly put on a chiffon top over her cotton trousers and almost ran out of her house. The drive to his house would normally take about an hour during rush hour, but because it was a Sunday, the roads were relatively empty. Aisha couldn't believe she was actually driving down to a house which had once been hers. So much water had flowed under the bridge since then.

When she got there, Raj Singh stood at the gate, helping her park the car just like old times. She looked around. The manicured lawns, beds of flowers, the two trees where Kabir used to tie his hammock—everything seemed the same. Only Raj Singh had aged. Not only was he looking old, but there was something in his demeanour which scared Aisha.

'Aap andar aiye, Madam,' Raj Singh was beating his chest and crying. 'Everything is over.'

Aisha rushed inside. The drawing room and the lobby looked the same.

'Mannu?' Aisha called out. She couldn't believe she was addressing him by the nickname she had chosen for him. What was wrong with her? Had she forgotten what she had suffered at his hands just a few years back?

'Mannu?' she called again as she gingerly opened the door of their erstwhile bedroom. He lay on the bed seemingly fast asleep, but something about his posture told her all was not well. A closer look and she saw it. He had bled profusely through his head. There was a gaping hole on one side and a pistol lay by his side. Mannu had been shot or had shot himself. But was that even possible?

Aisha's head was spinning. Raj Singh caught hold of her.

'Bibiji, I came to wake him up and saw this. I couldn't think of anything, so I called you. Sahab is no more, Bibiji,' the old man sobbed.

The enormity of the situation jolted Aisha into action. She fished out her mobile phone and dialled the number of the police station. Then she called the two numbers on her speed dial—Kabir, her son and Saima, her sister. She couldn't bring herself to tell them what had happened. All she could mutter was they needed to come immediately to the house at Palm Drive. She hoped and prayed they would understand. Kabir could get there faster—he lived in Dubai. Saima would take at least two days to reach since she lived on the other side of the globe. Aisha settled down on the sofa and asked Raj Singh to make her some strong coffee. The old man was glad to oblige.

Wave upon wave of memory assailed her as the past flashed before her in a kaleidoscope of images. They had met at an embassy party in London and befriended each other almost instantly. Their parents had met as well and an easy friendship had blossomed. Mannu or Mahendra Singh was every bit the eligible bachelor her parents had been looking for—a diplomat in the foreign services. And she was the cultured and beautiful bride the Singhs wanted for their only child. The two of them were married within the next three months.

The first few years were straight out of a Bollywood film. They travelled to beautiful locales, met new people and were doted upon by their families back home. Aisha was a journalist who had a flair for languages and she would try to learn as many new languages as possible. A few years down the line, they became parents to a lovely boy whom they named Kabir—a name inspired by a Sufi saint both of them admired.

When Kabir was in his early teens, Aisha felt it was time to focus on his studies so the family took the tough decision of living in separate places. Aisha stayed on at Palm Drive with her son while Mannu continued with his travels abroad. Aisha had taken to writing weekly columns for a local daily and this started to win her acclaim. Soon her pieces began to appear in some of the leading journals in the country. She was a keen observer, a great writer, and an empathetic journalist—a rarity in contemporary times.

It was also around this time that the skein of their marriage started to unravel and the couple realised with they preferred their own solitary spaces over their shared life. When Kabir turned eighteen, he moved to England for higher studies and Aisha saw no further reason to carry on with her marriage. They opted for a mutual divorce and it came through after the mandated period of separation. The only person who seemed to be really pained by this decision was Mannu's old aide, Raj Singh. Though his loyalties remained with his master and the old house, he could never forget Aisha. He had been extremely fond of her and coaxed her again and again to rethink. What Raj Singh hadn't realised was that Aisha had reached the end of her tether.

Mannu's indiscretions were legendary. A handsome man, he had a way with women. His suave persona coupled with his high-profile job made him extremely attractive to the opposite sex. Tired of the daily bickering over his infidelity, she had chosen to pack her bags and leave his house for good. This was almost a decade back. Since then, Mannu and Aisha had barely been in touch. If at all they communicated, it was through Kabir who called his father occasionally to check on him. There was no genuine attachment there, but a mere formality. Kabir, however, was extremely close to his mother and part of his disenchantment with his father was because of how badly he had treated his mother.

***

Aisha's head was reeling. She chose to lie down on the drawing room sofa. In spite of a pleasant summer morning, her teeth were chattering. The ever-solicitous Raj Singh covered her with a sheet and sat down on the floor next to her. They were waiting for day to break and whatever it would bring with it.

It was the press that got a whiff of this news first. Soon the driveway was full of reporters and cameramen who jostled for space and breaking news. For once, Aisha was happy to see the police. The young officer in command of the squad was respectful towards her. Being the ex-wife of the Ambassador had its uses. Mannu's body was carried out through the back entrance. Eerily, even the ambulance that drove him away was dead silent.

Aisha's mobile phone started ringing. The world had woken up to Ambassador Mahendra Singh's death as the media had gone live from the front gate of his residence. What a great story for the media, thought Aisha. A handsome dignified-looking man who had been a regular at all the high-society gatherings, an eminent guest at TV shows and a noted writer. Even the women around him made news—Mannu met and befriended some of the world's most beautiful women. But he was not just your average Casanova. Extremely well read, he had written books which had won him international acclaim.

Aisha was jolted back into the present by Raj Singh.

'Bibiji, please inform Kabir baba. He should not learn of Sahab's death through the television.'

Aisha felt tears welling up in her eyes. No, she wasn't shedding tears for her ex-husband. It was Raj Singh's concern for Kabir that moved her. She blinked them away as she tried to call her son yet again, but his phone was switched off. Maybe he had already boarded a flight. Aisha's head felt heavy. She wanted to sleep and never wake up. She curled up on the sofa and allowed her mind to drift away.

The next few days were a blur. Kabir had taken things in his own hands and for once, Aisha was happy to allow him to do so. The funeral, guest list, meeting with the police and the lawyers were being handled by Kabir. A stray thought struck Aisha—Kabir had hated his father. The last few years had seen a total breakdown of relationships but now he chatted with his father's friends, accepted condolences and even talked about his father's greatness as a statesman and parent.

Over the next few days, the house in Palm Drive was sealed, and the family shifted to Aisha's modest abode in Vasant Enclave. There was a constant stream of visitors from the highest echelons of society. Saima played the gracious hostess to perfection. She even gave bytes to TV channels and kept the home front moving like a well-oiled machine. Strangely, Mannu's death seemed to have united his worst enemies as now all three of them talked well about him. Since Mannu had not remarried and had no other family, Kabir was his sole heir. Was it the money or just plain etiquette that was bringing out the best in all of them?

To her shock, Aisha realised that after a very long time, she was feeling content and happy. In the public eye, she was still diplomat Manvendra's wife. It was as if the divorce had never happened. The press was reporting favourably about the diplomat, talking about his numerous accomplishments. The bitterness that had made his name unmentionable in Aisha's family circle earlier had ebbed, as if in his death, Mannu had been exonerated. Even in her mind, Aisha only revisited the happy times spent with him. Sometimes, it even brought a smile to her face. Kabir seemed content and even Saima who had been Mannu's worst critic found good things to say about him. As a rule, the suicide was not discussed between the three of them. The thought had worried Aisha, but Kabir had put her mind to rest.

'It's okay, Mom. Dad is no more. Let's not pry into his privacy. From the looks of it, he was a lonely man. Maybe his loneliness killed him.'

'But then it's our fault Kabir—yours and mine. Maybe we should have met him more often.'

'No, Mom. It's not our fault. We were just a phone call away. Dad could have reached out. Anyway, there is no use pondering over it. We need to move on.'

And move on they did. After the funeral and the prayer meet, Kabir still had a few days free. He took his mother and aunt on a weekend break to a resort in the foothills of the Himalayas. He wanted his mother and aunt to relax. The sisters giggled like school girls and Saima even went on a pony ride. Kabir clicked photographs on his phone which he shared with Saima's family in the US. He called up his cousins on a video chat and the entire family laughed and talked about what Saima's girls termed 'the oldies' desperate bid for childhood'. It was as if Mannu's death had washed away the years of sorrow that the family had been forced to grapple with. Now they were back to being who they used to be once upon a time.

They were back in the time before the divorce happened, before Mannu slapped her and drove her out of the house, before the rounds of lawyers, before Kabir ran away from the country to escape his father's tales of debauchery. It had been an eternity, but now it was over. Aisha had survived it and done well for herself. She had even managed to shelve his memories...or had she?

Soon, Aisha's life got back to the old routine. The only new addition was a visit to the house at Palm Drive once a month to give Raj Singh enough money to keep the place in order. Kabir had talked to the property dealers and the house would be soon up for sale. Raj Singh was very happy each time Aisha visited. He would make her favourite dishes and ensure she was well cared for. Aisha appreciated his efforts, but refused to go live in the house. It was too big and unwieldy and the memories of Mannu made it difficult for her to call the place her own.

***

The telephone was ringing again. It was Aisha's yoga time so she chose to ignore it. She made a mental note to keep the phone off the hook when she was doing her yoga. For a minute, it stopped ringing, but sprang back to life again. She muttered a curse under her breath as she took the call.

'Aisha, I'm Saba. We were at journalism college together. Remember me? I need to see you urgently.'

Aisha remembered Saba well—she was quite a firebrand at college, courting controversies for her revolutionary views. Aisha had followed her work for almost a decade in the first phase of her career. Saba was a fearless journalist and her newspaper columns had been extremely popular, but that was a long time ago. In recent times, she had not read anything of hers. She was quite surprised Saba had called. They hadn't exactly been friends.

'I remember you Saba but what is this about?'

'Your husband. I have some information about him. It's urgent.'

Aisha was bewildered. In three decades of knowing each other, Saba had never reached out to her. Before Aisha could ask more questions, Saba disconnected the phone after telling her where they should meet. Aisha sank into the sofa and covered her face. Mannu would not allow her to live in peace. The shadow of the man had eclipsed her life completely, but she would battle on for herself and her son.

Saba looked much older than what Aisha had thought. She wore a no-nonsense salwar kameez, a dupatta and huge glasses that covered half her face. Her hair was greying in parts and she seemed to have made no attempt at colouring it. Aisha disliked her immediately. She had no patience for women who let themselves go. Personal grooming mattered. In spite of the distasteful task she was doing at the moment, Aisha flaunted a well-tailored pant suit. Her hair was neat—every strand in place and her Hermès scarf and hand bag beautifully accessorised her attire. Saba seemed to be completely unimpressed by Aisha's attire or looks. She gulped down the tea she had ordered and came to the point.

'Your ex-husband was a disgusting man. It's good he killed himself or else he would have been murdered by one of his women.'

Every pore in Aisha's body revolted. 'And who gives you the right to speak of my husband like that?'

'Ex-husband, you mean,' Saba was quick with her rejoinder.

'Exactly why have you called me here? The man is dead and I'm not keen to discuss him with you or anybody else. What do you want from me?'

Saba pulled out her business card from her bag and slid it across the table towards Aisha.

'I'm a journalist who has been independently investigating your husband's death. It's not been easy. With the clout you all have, the police was happy to close the case. The mainstream media picked up the story initially and then mysteriously dropped it. In their later reportage, they almost made him out to be a saint.'

'But why are you telling me all this? I had nothing to do with the media or the police,' Aisha retorted angrily. It had been a mistake coming out to meet this woman alone. She should have known better and got the family lawyer along.

'Your son did,' Saba's voice was steady.

'What!' Aisha almost choked on her tea. She wasn't going to take this anymore. She stood up.

'Your son, with the help of Mr. Subramanyam. I'm not sure who helped whom, but the story was buried in a day's time.'

Aisha was confused. Subby was a family friend. He had been there with them throughout the traumatic phase and yes, he also happened to be an influential person in the government.

'I didn't call you here to traumatise you, Aisha,' Saba's tone was soothing. 'I thought I could talk to you since I have followed your writings for over two decades now. You have written fearlessly and with feeling, and always steered clear of your ex-husband's politics.'

'What do you want from me?' Aisha's voice trembled as if she was facing her worst fears—something she had willed herself to run away from. Something inside her told her Saba was telling the truth but she couldn't let down her guard—not so soon anyway.

'Aisha, what I'm going to tell you won't be easy on you. I know that you have been through a lot and have now created a very dignified and productive space for yourself. I wouldn't have come to you had I not seen your work at the NGO and read your fearless writing…'

Aisha realised Saba was trying to pacify her, but that made her more edgy. Something sinister seemed to be afoot.

'Aisha, he has a daughter.' Saba reached out and held Aisha's hand.

For days after that, Aisha played this scene over and over in her mind. Saba's story had sounded real and unreal all at once. Saba didn't seem to be lying—at least Aisha didn't see any reason for her to lie.

Aisha had known all along that Mannu had a roving eye. It was his indiscretions which had resulted in their divorce. Yet, sitting in the coffee shop and listening to the tale about his dalliance with a typist who used to visit their house made Aisha want to throw up.

Saba had been following certain officers in the government over a case of financial bungling. Her search had narrowed down to Mahendra Singh who had just returned from a foreign posting. She was to shadow him for years and had become privy to his innumerable indiscretions as a married man and later, as a single man. He had met the typist Meena in his office and later, Meena started to accompany him home for doing typing work. Aisha remembered Meena clearly—she was a quiet person who remained mostly at her desk in Mannu's study. To even think Mannu could have liked her felt like an abomination, particularly since his arm candies used to be beautiful socialites.

But Saba had copious notes on where they met, photographs of them together and of course, if Saba was to be believed—there was also the daughter named Priya. Apparently, Mannu was quite devoted to this family and had proved to be a loving father. The child was around two years old when Mannu was transferred to the US. This was also the time when Meena was diagnosed with cancer—she was to pass away soon after.

Mannu had flown to India to attend her funeral. Aisha had appreciated the gesture then, since it reflected Mannu's concern for his staff. She remembered him being distracted for days thereafter—Aisha had attributed it to the shock of seeing a person you had known closely dying an untimely death. She had never suspected that Meena had left behind a daughter.

Little Priya had grown up with her grandmother in Kasauli and done her schooling in Shimla. Mannu had continued to support the family through Raj Singh, his trusted aide. That Raj Singh had known everything and had kept it a secret from her, felt like a worse betrayal than what she had suffered at the hands of her ex-husband. Priya was now a college-going girl and the grandmother was no more.

'Why tell me all this now?' Aisha asked in a tortured voice, looking Saba in the eye.

'Believe me, Aisha, I have thought this through. Manvendra caused you enough pain and just when you have made peace with the world, I am probably bringing it crashing down. But I had no choice. I have followed Manvendra's second family closely, I saw little Priya grow up without her parents. And now the only person she had in this world is dead. The girl has no one to call her own. I don't expect you to adopt her— she is too independent to allow it anyway. Aisha, I have followed your trajectory closely, your writing, your initiative in taking up gender issues...I just thought you would understand. The choice is entirely yours— you can treat this as a figment of my imagination or meet Priya and see where this new relationship takes you. I felt I owed this to Meena who I used to know reasonably well. Priya is a good kid. You might like her.' Saba stood up.

Aisha rose too. 'One last question Saba, how did my husband die?'

'Oh! That's simple. He killed himself. His debts were mounting and he was barely able to sustain the luxurious lifestyle he was used to. It was also loneliness, I guess—for the last three years or so he had no company except Raj Singh. Manvendra Singh was used to a larger-than-life existence and when that started dissipating, he lost the will to live.'

Saba gave Aisha a quick hug before she left.

***

Aisha couldn't believe what was happening to her. A tsunami had wrecked her newfound peace and she was back to where she had started. This time she did not have Kabir or Saima as her allies—she had chosen to keep this information to herself. Three months had passed since her chat with Saba. The latter had called a couple of times, but Aisha had remained aloof and unfriendly.

Then Saba had texted she was leaving for Kabul on a UN assignment and would be off the radar for a while. That was the last Aisha had heard from her.

Aisha tried hard to forget, but she could not get the picture of an ailing Meena cuddling a small child out of her mind.

Months passed and it was time for the Spring Festival at JJ University. The festival was meant to bring out the creative streak in the students through competitions in dramatics, music and debates.

Flower shows and talent rounds and a carnivalesque atmosphere dominated the campus for a week. Every year, Aisha, an alumna, would be invited as a judge or guest speaker. She enjoyed her time there—it made her feel young. This year, she did not feel like attending it, but she had committed to it months back. A last-minute cancellation would be unprofessional. She remembered Saba mentioning Priya studied there and lived on campus in one of the hostels.

In spite of her misgivings, she showed up. Her talk was a great success. Students gathered around her, asking for her contact details. It made Aisha happy to think that these young men and women read her works and wanted to emulate her. When she was leaving, two students accompanied her to her car. They carried the bouquet and the memento she had been gifted at the event. They shook hands with her politely as they introduced themselves.

'I'm Armaan and this is Priya. We are the coordinators for Utkarsh.' The young man said.

'Utkarsh is the name of our Journalism Society,' the girl piped up. 'Ma'am, I've heard a lot about you from Saba Khala. She was my mother's friend. She said you both went to the same journalism school as us.'

Aisha's head was spinning as she settled back in her car. The entire day's event fizzled out as her head reverberated with words like 'Priya', 'Saba Khala' and 'Mother's friend'. Her mind was in a turmoil. She felt the onset of a migraine even as she heard herself tell the driver, 'Take me to Palm Drive.' She had no idea why she said this or what she intended to do. Suddenly, it seemed imperative to find out the truth from the one man who knew it all, but had continued to remain the keeper of his master's secrets.

Raj Singh was evasive and denied any knowledge of Priya till Aisha threatened to remove him from his services. Finally, he broke down, sought her forgiveness, but was loath to share any information. Yes, he had been aware of Sahabji's fondness for Meena. He had tried to prevent her from coming home to work, but Sahab hadn't listened. He had been hopeful that Aisha would figure out what was going on and would put a stop to it.

'So, it was my fault, Raj Singh?' Aisha was furious.

'Not your fault, Bibiji, but you were always busy with Kabir baba or your computer.'

'I am a journalist; I had work to do, Raj Singh.' Aisha's voice was cold as ice.

'Yes, wasn't it your job too to hold your family together? You never gave Sahab any importance. He was such a great man. You were always busy; it was always about yourself.' Raj Singh's voice was choking with emotion; there were tears in his eyes. For the first time in the three decades that Aisha had known him, he was speaking his mind.

'Sahab spent a lot of money on them, Bibiji. Meena was a jadugarni. She had bewitched Sahab with her politeness and good manners. Her daughter was born in a big hospital—all expenses paid by Sahab. She studied in Shimla in a very beautiful school. Sahab was very partial towards her. He never went to see her himself, but used to send me. When Meena died, Sahab attended her funeral.'

'Who does the girl live with now?' Aisha asked.

'I don't know, Bibiji. I used to see her when she was in school and later, when she came to live with her grandmother in Kasauli. Sahab had created a trust for her, and her grandmother was to take care of it till she came of age. There's enough money for the girl, Bibiji.'

'Raj Singh, I had the highest regard for you because I thought you cared for Kabir and me. But you allowed Mannu to get away with his flings, and you never spared a thought for Meena or the poor motherless girl. I want you to pack and leave right away. Your money will be sent to your home along with a generous pension to see you through.'

With that, Aisha turned around and left. When she got home and switched on her laptop, she saw that there were several mails from the students of JJ University. Normally these mails would make her happy and she would answer most of them but she deleted all of them. There was one from Priya as well telling her how much she had admired her speech. Aisha pressed the delete button hard willing all the mails to disappear. She didn't ever want hear these offending names. She made a mental note to never visit JJ University and blocked all the IDs from which the mails had been sent, as if by blocking mails, she would be free of the guilt and pain which had overcome her. She started sleeping poorly, and coming down with migraines; her well-crafted daily schedule began to crumble, paving the way for melancholy and despair.

Two torturous months passed. Aisha was yet to settle back into her old routine. That night, she was winding up her video chat with Kabir and about to call it a day. Dona, her live-in maid, had served her a cup of herbal tea and retired for the night. Aisha wasn't sleepy so she turned on the TV and was channel surfing lazily when the bold headlines of a news channel made her sit up straight. JJ University was under attack. Goons had entered the University and were beating up students. There were videos of students bleeding as they ran around looking for shelter. Some of them seemed badly hurt.

Aisha couldn't believe her eyes. She reached out for her mobile phone and started to check her Twitter feed. It was all over Twitter too. Some journalists were reporting live from there and the students trapped inside were appealing for help. Aisha was assailed by multiple emotions—her alma mater was under attack and she needed to stand by it. But there was a bigger force propelling her, even though she didn't want to acknowledge it. She quickly pulled on a pair of jeans and a jacket, laced up her running shoes and rushed to her car. Dona came out on to the balcony, confused. Her mistress never went out at night—what exactly was going on? Aisha waved to her and asked her to go inside. She started the car and drove at top speed to the University gates.

There was a large crowd there comprising students, professors, the press and concerned parents. A big posse of police personnel was manning the gates. They weren't letting anyone inside. Aisha ran to the nearest police woman.

'Please Ma'am, allow me to go in. My…my girl is in there.'

'Which hostel?' The seemingly sympathetic police woman asked.

Aisha had no idea so she said the first name that came to mind. 'Vivekananda Hostel.'

'Oh! That's safe. Students haven't been harmed there.'

'See, I'm also from the press. In my haste, I forgot my ID card. Please let me in,' Aisha begged.

'Sorry, we can't do that. But we are evacuating the hostels. You can keep waiting here. Your daughter will be brought outside safely.'

Aisha winced at the word 'daughter', but was somewhat relieved when she heard the word 'safely'. Maybe she was panicking unnecessarily. Probably the students were indeed safe. The trouble was she had no idea where Priya lived. She had never asked and didn't know she cared.

Aisha joined the other parents as they waited for their children to be brought out. It was a bitterly cold night. Not only did Aisha manage to hold out, she also consoled parents who would break down from time to time.

'Don't worry, our children will be safe. It's going to be alright,' she heard herself say.

Slowly and steadily, the students walked out of the University gates in a single file. Some met their families; others tried to connect with them on their mobile phones. Ambulances blared loudly on their way out with the injured, while the police tried to bring the situation under control.

'Aisha Ma'am! What brings you here?' It was Armaan, the young boy who had come to see her off after the talk.

'Priya? Your friend Priya. Is she alright?'

If Armaan was surprised, he didn't show it. 'Yes Ma'am, she is right there,' he said pointing at Priya who was escorting an injured friend into a waiting car.

Aisha ran in her direction.

'Priya,' she called out.

Priya smiled back. 'Thanks for being here, Aisha Ma'am. I hope you have been covering the events here. We need the press to hear our story.'

Aisha smiled. 'Actually, I came because of you.'

Seeing the young girl's confused expression, she added, 'Your Saba Khala asked me to.' Well, that wasn't a complete lie.

'Oh! I know Saba Khala went to Kabul on some UN mission. It's so nice of her to have contacted you. She has always watched out for me.'

'Yes, you are special to Saba,' Aisha smiled. 'I want you to come home with me.'

'I can't. My friends are here. I can't leave them.'

'Bring them along. I have a small house, but all of you can squeeze in.'

Soon Aisha was driving back with five young men and women in her car. They were talking excitedly about what had happened, briefing Aisha on the attack and what followed. They were indignant and angry and hoping strict action would be taken against the perpetrators. She shared their anguish and promised to write about the event in the leading newspaper she wrote for.

Aisha settled them in her two bedrooms. They were grateful for her hospitality and apologetic for putting her through this trouble. Aisha felt a strange kind of happiness at having them around. It seemed to fill her whole being. She settled on her drawing room sofa, covered herself with a quilt. That night, she took the landline off the hook and also remembered to put her mobile phone on silent mode.

9

Deliverance

Jyotsna pushed and pushed. Her entire body was bathed in sweat and her agony knew no bounds, but the baby was not ready to enter the world yet. Jyotsna's mother sat outside the labour room, praying hard for her young daughter.

'Please, Ma Kali, have mercy on her, she is all of eighteen. Please, Ma, I suffered everything you put me through. Don't let Jyotsna go through the same hell. Please, Ma, let a son be born to her.'

Ruma had been widowed at the tender age of twenty. Jyotsna had been just a few months old at the time. After her husband's sudden death, Ruma had found herself at the mercy of her in-laws. She was beaten up on the slightest pretext and held responsible for her husband's demise. She was called a witch who had polluted the house. Married women avoided her for fear that her bad luck would rub off on them. Ruma hadn't protested against all the indignities heaped on her. In her heart of hearts, she knew she must be at fault. She must have done something terribly wrong to have merited her suffering.

Born to parents who were poor farmers, she had been married off before her fifteenth birthday. Luckily, her husband had been a kind man. He had waited for her to grow up a bit before he took her. This annoyed her in-laws immensely and they had called her a witch who had cast a spell on their son. Her husband had kept quiet, allowing his mother to abuse him, but he had not taken Ruma to bed. Ruma had slowly learnt to love him and when they finally slept together, it was something she cherished.

Ruma was a shy girl. She could not talk about her happiness to anyone, but it was clear in the way she was blossoming into a beautiful woman. When she was pregnant with Jyotsna, her husband ensured she was well taken care of. He would scold his mother and sister if they asked her to do any hard physical labour. Ruma was too shy to protest. She bashfully acknowledged her husband's love by taking care of all his needs. He had grown to love his 'little wife' just as she had grown to love him.

One night, after gently making love to her, he told her that he was planning to leave the village for the city, and that he would take her along. He was just waiting for their child to be born before he informed his parents. Ruma's eyes filled with tears of gratitude. What more could she ask for? She thanked Ma Kali as she quietly lay by his side. She could feel the baby kicking inside her and smiled.

***

Jyotsna screamed again.

'Don't panic my girl. Everything will be fine. You will have a Baal Gopal next to you soon,' Ruma consoled her daughter.

Having battled life all alone, Ruma had been very protective about her daughter. She tried to do everything in her power to make Jyotsna happy. She had sent Jyotsna to school. Jyotsna was a good student and she was also a pretty girl, justifying the name her father had given her. He had told Ruma their daughter was as beautiful as moonlight. And moonlight she truly was—glowing, looking more and more beautiful by the day.

One day, Mrs. Chatterjee approached Ruma.

'What are your plans for Jyotsna?' she asked.

Ruma bent low to touch her feet. Mrs. Chatterjee was the matriarch of a prosperous family and the owner of a large clothes factory. It was she who had saved Ruma's life by enrolling her into a sewing class and later, by giving her a job in the factory. Ruma lived in the factory quarters and had single-handedly brought up Jyotsna. She had nursed a dream—of educating her daughter so that Jyotsna could become a doctor, a profession for which Ruma had the highest regard.

***

Jyotsna cried out in agony. Ruma dabbed her head with a cloth. The girl was sweating profusely. Suddenly, there was a flurry in the hospital corridors as Mrs. Chatterjee and her brother Shomu walked in. Ruma stood up in deference. In spite of her pain, Jyotsna tried hard to cover her head, but failed.

'It's alright, Bou,' Mrs. Chatterjee said with a touch of authority. 'Rama, I have informed the doctors. She will be well taken care of. I pray it will be a boy.'

The last sentence sounded more like an order.

Shomu stepped dangerously close to Jyotsna's bed and whispered sinisterly, 'I want a son. Bou, can you hear me?'

Ruma could feel Jyotsna trembling with fear.

***

Ruma had worked for sixteen to eighteen hours a day. Her body had acquired a strange stoop from sitting in front of the sewing machine for hours. Her fingers had thickened and there were blisters on them. But Ruma was happy. Her work was appreciated in the factory and she had been able to enroll her daughter in a good school. She had also managed to arrange tuitions for her. Jyotsna was a diligent student and Masterbabu, her home tutor, praised her to the skies.

Shyamji was an old man who had taken a liking to the mother-daughter duo. After the tuitions, he would sit down with a steaming cup of tea and tell them stories about the goings-on in the world. These were Ruma's favourite moments. She learnt so much from him. Shyamji treated Ruma with utmost respect, addressing her as his Chhotoma. Jyotsna called him Dadu. Dadu opened Jyotsna's mind to the world, and both mother and daughter felt a kindred spirit was lifting them up and setting them free. In Dadu's world, there was no difference between the rich and the poor, nor was there anything a woman couldn't achieve. Together, they dreamt of Jyotsna growing up to become a famous doctor.

***

'Ma, what if it's not a boy?' Jyotsna muttered through gritted teeth. The pain had started to torment her again.

Ruma continued to dab her head with a cloth.

***

The day Jyotsna cleared her twelfth boards with distinction, there was celebration in Ruma's modest one-room quarter. She had invited Masterbabu and three of his other students for dinner. She had cooked some fish and mutton and also made payesh. Her guests ate heartily and praised her cooking skills. Heady with happiness, Ruma had bought some new fabric from the market and sewn Jyotsna her first salwar kameez. For someone who had grown up wearing frocks made of leftover cut pieces from the factory in which Ruma worked, this was a huge treat. Jyotsna spread out her hands and did a little pirouette.

Jyotsna's college was far away. Ruma spent all her savings to buy a cycle for her. Jyotsna cycled ten kilometres a day to her college. At first, Ruma was a little scared to let her go, but Masterbabu had been insistent. She began to take pride in seeing her girl riding to school in a white salwar kameez, with her hair in two plaits, tied neatly with white ribbons.

The girl was a beauty. Ruma had already started getting marriage proposals for Jyotsna, but each time she said a firm no. Her daughter was destined for better things. She would realise her mother's dream of becoming a doctor one day. Even the thought of it filled Ruma's heart with untold joy. No, her girl would not suffer the same fate as her. She would live up to Masterbabu's dreams.

***

'Water...' moaned Jyotsna, cutting into Ruma's dreams. She held her daughter close as the latter gulped down some water. The pain had become even more severe and Jyotsna's entire being seemed to be contracting with its intensity.

'Ma, they'll kill me if it's not a boy,' Jyotsna rasped.

'Don't worry. Nothing of the sort will happen,' Ruma's voice sounded hollow. She knew the power the Chatterjees wielded in the village.

'Someone is following me,' Jyotsna had reported a couple of months ago, after returning from college one day. Ruma was worried. She didn't allow her daughter to go to college for a few days. Then the much-awaited summer vacation arrived and both mother and daughter forgot about the incident. Once

Jyotsna went back to college, a man followed her around on a motorbike. Jyotsna was petrified, but she knew missing college would only add to her woes. She needed to spend time in the library after classes. It would be late evening by the time she would return home. Most often she would be alone.

Then one day, her stalker accosted her. Holding her in a vice-like grip he led her to the fields. Jyotsna was too shocked to protest. He fondled her and kissed her like a madman. He said he loved her and wished to marry her. In her bid to get away, Jyotsna ran back home, forgetting her cycle which lay in the fields as helpless and broken as her. The dreaded man was none other than Shomu, Mrs. Chatterjee's brother, a man in his late thirties who was known for his misdeeds. In the village, he walked around with the swagger of a man who knew he could have anything because his sister had the money and clout. Shomu insisted on getting married to Jyotsna right away.

Within days, the marriage was solemnised. Ruma's friends at the sewing centre held her hand, allowing her to weep her heart out. They wiped their faces clean the moment they saw Mrs. Chatterjee. She was the person who put bread on their table. No one dared say anything to her and her brother. Deep down, everybody knew Jyotsna's life would be worse than hell. There was no crime Shomu had not been accused of. From highway robbery to dacoity to rape, he had done it all. He had been accused of many crimes, but nothing could ever be proved against him. He had gone underground for a few years after a murder charge had surfaced, but now he was back and his gaze had fallen on the pretty Jyotsna.

Jyotsna dreaded the night when Shomu would take her with animal ferocity. His bestiality knew no bounds. Jyotsna tried everything in her power to end her misery. Running away didn't work; this was followed by a couple of failed suicide attempts.

As part of her punishment, she was beaten black and blue and left to starve. Her rebellion ended when she became pregnant and realised she was truly at Shomu's mercy. Her body had grown big and lethargic and had refused to cooperate with her. It was as if it was someone else's body which had been tasked with producing a male heir for the Chatterjee family. In spite of her hatred for Shomu and Mrs. Chatterjee, Jyotsna had started to love the baby growing inside her. 'You're mine. I'll protect you,' she would whisper to her unborn child. She now understood why her mother would go to any lengths to protect her.

***

Jyotsna felt her body quickening and pulsating as the pain tore through her. And then, with a final push, her task was done. She was faintly conscious when she heard her baby crying and managed to smile weakly when she realised she had performed the task allocated to her. God had been kind. Jyotsna had given birth to a male child.

Wild celebrations followed soon after. Everyone in the hospital was thanked and rewarded in cash and kind by Mrs. Chatterjee. The doctor was gifted a spanking new car. Drummers beat their drums till the wee hours of the morning as Shomu and his friends danced. Cartons of beer were downed and the entire village joined in the celebration. Overnight, Ruma and Jyotsna had become mini celebrities as everyone came to congratulate the mother and daughter.

Mrs. Chatterjee took off her thick gold chain and put it around Jyotsna's neck. Shomu went a step further and kissed his wife in full public view. And then, with a flourish he told her, 'What do you want from me, Bou? Whatever you ask for will be yours.'

In a shaky voice, Jyotsna muttered, 'I want to spend some time with my mother in her house.' After expressing her wish, the young mother fell back on her pillow, exhausted after the long and gruelling day.

Mrs. Chatterjee took her brother to task the minute she could talk to him in private.

'Who asked you to show such kindness? Don't you know these small people always tend to take advantage? First, you find a lowlife to get married to and now you even want her to stay with her mother in the coolie quarters! You'll drag my good name to the ashes.'

But Shomu had already given his word in public and could not go back on it now. So after her stay in the hospital, Jyotsna went to her mother's house.

The 'house' was a meagre tin shed with some space in the front where Jyotsna had planted a few flowering plants. The flowers had bloomed as if they had anticipated Jyotsna's homecoming. This was the first time in three long years that she was visiting her childhood home. Shomu had ensured she could not visit her poor mother. Occasionally, Ruma would come visiting, but in the sprawling Chatterjee bungalow, she was treated like an unwanted servant.

The mother and daughter barely met. On the few occasions when Ruma visited, Mrs. Chatterjee would plant someone in Jyotsna's room to make sure the mother and daughter could not speak freely to each other.

Now, Jyotsna clung to her mother and wept her heart out. There was so much to talk about, so much to share and they barely had time—just a week before she would go back to her marital home, a place she detested with all her heart.

Shomu was a brute in his demeanour and in bed. Every night, he tore into Jyotsna like a mad bull. In the initial days, Jyotsna could hardly bear the pain, but slowly she had schooled her body to put up with his atrocities without complaining. Her pliant nature had met with his approval though the physical abuse continued unabated. That stopped only when she became pregnant as it was a belief in the Chatterjee house that having intercourse with a pregnant woman brought disaster in its wake. The men were free to seek satisfaction elsewhere, but their wives were out of bounds till childbirth. Jyotsna had heaved a sigh of relief; the focus of her life had become her unborn child.

Jyotsna and Ruma cried more than they talked. Both realised they were powerless against the Chatterjees. Jyotsna too was a mother now and she knew how her heart fluttered each time her son cried. Waking up to motherhood she realised she could not run away. Where would she go with her baby? What if he died of hunger? What if the Chatterjees took him away from her?

Aware of this herself, Ruma pleaded with her daughter to make peace with her situation.

'Do as they say, child. At no point must you annoy your husband. Do as your mother-in-law instructs you. They will take care of you now. You have given them an heir, the coveted male child.' Yet, her inner being was screaming, 'Run away from them, Jyotsna. As far as you can. Don't bother with the bastard Shomu or the baby. After all, he too will take after his father.'

Seven days went by in a flash. Jyotsna's body was still weak from childbirth. Ruma was too poor and helpless to even try to help Jyotsna. All she could do was pray hard for her daughter and the baby. 'Ma Kali, please protect the girl. I will do everything to propitiate you. Please, Ma. My daughter has never hurt even a fly. Why have you reserved such a terrible fate for her?'

When it was time, the Chatterjees sent their driver to pick up Jyotsna and the baby. That was a rare honour. Jyotsna had never had the luxury of sitting in the car. Even when she was about to deliver the baby, Mrs. Chatterjee had had her dropped to the hospital in a rickshaw accompanied by a maid. It had been a bumpy ride. The rickshaw puller had been cautious and tried his best to make it comfortable for the heavily pregnant girl, but the makeshift earthen road in the village was full of potholes which had filled up with water after the previous night's rain.

Mrs. Chatterjee never passed up an opportunity to remind Jyotsna about where she had come from. She might have married her brother, but the girl was not allowed to forget that she was an unwanted appendage in the prosperous Chatterjee household.

Ruma hugged her daughter one last time as Jyotsna sat in the car with her baby on her lap, and wept bitterly. Jyotsna's face was covered with her sari so no one could tell what the girl was going through. Her body shook with unshed tears, but she was careful not to let them drop. Her mother had cautioned her that if a mother's tears fell on her baby, it would bring him bad luck.

It was a ten-minute drive from her mother's quarters to the Chatterjee household. Even in the midst of her misery, the young girl could not help but register the luxury of sitting in a car. It felt as if she was flying, with the roads and trees melting before her eyes. A pleasant breeze blew away her sari and she looked at the familiar village with new eyes.

The baby woke up and stared at his mother intently. 'I will take care of you son. I won't let them win,' Jyotsna muttered as the car slowly wound its way into the large driveway of the Chatterjee household.

Something had definitely changed in the Chatterjee household. Jyotsna was no longer the unwanted girl whom everyone tolerated because of Shomu. Being mother to the heir apparent had raised her worth. Shomu started to treat her with a degree of kindness and Mrs. Chatterjee's barbs lessened. The servants too seemed kinder. The Chatterjee household didn't seem as unbearable as it had been earlier.

Little Gopal was the apple of Mrs. Chatterjee's eyes and her tolerance for Jyotsna increased when the family priest predicted great things for the boy and also complimented the young mother, saying she would beget more male children for the family.

Gopal was growing up quite fast. He was a bright baby with a healthy appetite. He kept his mother engaged throughout the day with his numerous demands. Jyotsna barely had any time for herself. Household chores and caring for her child took a toll on her health. Her face was still beautiful, but she was almost skeletal and didn't look like she was in any condition to bear more children for Shomu. Mrs. Chatterjee was tiring of her and threatened to send her away and get another girl from a good family for Shomu.

'I don't know what my brother saw in you. Your mother and you are not fit to be our servants, but look at my misfortune, I have to treat you like an equal.'

Jyotsna would keep her head down as tears streamed down her cheeks. On other occasions, Mrs. Chatterjee would threaten to throw her out of the house once she stopped breastfeeding her little boy. Mrs. Chatterjee felt the boy would have a much better upbringing if he grew up without his mother who didn't qualify to be a part of their affluent household.

Jyotsna knew she had exhausted all her reasons to live, but even suicide was not an option available to her now. She shuddered to think of her child growing up without his mother. Time and again, she planned her escape from the Chatterjee mansion, but the idea was abandoned even as it took root. Where would she go with her baby? Worse still, what would they do her mother once they found out what she had done? That only left her exhausted, pained and disillusioned. Over time, it became clear to her—hers was an entrapment from which there was no escape.

The thought was so depressing that Jyotsna started to slowly relinquish her hold on life. She barely communicated while her body slowly wasted away.

Help came from unforeseen quarters. The lady doctor at the dispensary had been tasked with the routine job of checking on little Gopal. She visited the Chatterjee household once in a while to ensure the wellness of the coveted heir of the Chatterjee family. The only outsider who was allowed to enter Jyotsna's room and spend some time there, she advised the young mother on the child's inoculation, diet and other sundry things. A maid was always present on such occasions since Mrs. Chatterjee never trusted Jyotsna with an outsider. In the early days, Jyotsna would look forward to the doctor's visit—she was her only connection with the world outside. But now that Jyotsna had lost her will to live, she stared at the doctor uncomprehendingly, barely making an effort to register what she said.

'Shobhita, go and fetch some milk. Do it right now,' the doctor's voice was sharp as she addressed the maid. Her voice carried so much authority that Shobhita rushed to the kitchen to get some milk.

The doctor held Jyotsna by her shoulder and looked her in the eye. 'I know everything about you, my girl. I know you wanted to study and become a doctor. All is not lost yet. You need to have faith. Also, remember to take this medicine every day without fail.'

Shobhita was back with a steaming glass of milk.

'Make Jyotsna drink that milk. She has to drink a glass of it every day. The baby is doing perfectly fine, but if you don't take care of the mother, she won't survive,' the doctor ordered.

'I will come back soon, Jyotsna. Make sure you follow every word I have told you.' The doctor's gaze held Jyotsna's for a few seconds before she turned and walked out of the door.

Jyotsna was confused. How did the doctor know these details about her? Had she met her mother or Masterbabu? Something in her heart was singing and bringing her back to life—it was the hope of seeing Doctor Didi again. Jyotsna would wait for her visits.

The next time Doctor Didi visited, she brought with her some birth control pills and a form for open-schooling. She managed to get rid of the maid for a longish period and talked at length to Jyotsna. Yes, she knew her mother from her medical rounds in the factory. Ruma had confided in her and sought her help. Since the mother was not allowed to meet the daughter, it was only Doctor Didi who could do something. Ruma had confided in her that Jyotsna had been a very bright student and had won scholarships. But the chance encounter with Shomu had played havoc with her life.

Jyotsna's eyes brightened at the thought of being with her books once again, but her face clouded instantly—the Chatterjees would never allow it. It was unthinkable.

Doctor Didi was reassuring. 'Fill up your form and let me see how things play out. I will talk to your mother-in-law. Have faith in me.'

Convincing Mrs. Chatterjee wasn't easy. The doctor played on her pride, praising her to the skies, telling her how she was a role model for every woman in the village. She had allowed her brother to marry a poor woman of a lower caste. If she allowed Jyotsna to study, she would go down in history as one of the most progressive women in Basantapur Ilaka. For all you knew, a statue of hers may be erected near mandirtala.

The flattery worked. Mrs. Chatterjee allowed Jyotsna to complete her education. The restrictions were still in place—she would not be allowed to go out of the house; she could only meet people with the mistress's permission; she would have to do her household chores and after all this, if time permitted, she could study.

For Jyotsna, this was manna from heaven. She wept, holding her books in her hands—it had been so long. It was as if her lifeblood had been returned to her. She blossomed again, and though handling the household chores, taking care of her demanding child and managing to find time for her studies was Herculean, she held on.

Shomu wasn't happy with Mrs. Chatterjee's decision. He took it out on Jyotsna, beating her black and blue on several occasions, but Jyotsna had learnt to bear with it. She didn't complain. She was happy Shomu had a girl in town whom he visited quite often. She had heard Mrs. Chatterjee rebuking Shomu for this, but for Jyotsna it proved to be a blessing. She devoted the nights to her studies, making copious notes and remembering to hide them before her drunk husband got back. Life was a roller coaster and soon it was time for her exams.

Shobhita and the guard accompanied Jyotsna to the examination centre. Every day, she saw her mother looking at her from the other side of the street. The women did not acknowledge each other, but Jyotsna could feel her mother's blessings reaching her even as tears clouded her vision. A determined Jyotsna took her exams—she knew this was the chance of a lifetime, and she could not fritter it away. A couple of months later when the results were declared, not only had Jyotsna cleared her exams with distinction, but she was also declared the district topper.

Mrs. Chatterjee went to receive the award on Jyotsna's behalf and delivered a speech about being an emancipated woman. The award was kept in a special place in the drawing room. Both Shomu and his sister pointed it out to their guests, emphasising their role in having allowed a poor girl to become part of their family and then allowing her to study. The guests went back praising the Chatterjees to high heaven.

Jyotsna did not know what was being said or discussed. Once in a while, she got to touch her award when she came in to do the dusting and cleaning. Jyotsna's mind was now occupied with other things. She wanted to get a job—any job that would take her far away. She now had a degree and was willing to do anything to be able to stand on her own feet. Again, Doctor Didi helped her fill up the applications and apply to schools across the country.

It was an agonising six months wait before Jyotsna received a call. A school in Kolkata was looking for a pre-nursery teacher. The salary was very low, but they would allow her to stay in the teacher's quarters within the compound.

Jyotsna's mind was made up. She was determined to move there with her mother and her child. She would take up the job. This time, subterfuge wouldn't work, so she decided to talk to Shomu once he was back from one of his escapades in town.

'I have a job offer. Can I take it up? I will take Gopal with me. I will admit him to a school there. Schools there are very good. We will both come back every weekend. It's hardly any distance from here.'

Jyotsna kept her head down as she mumbled. She didn't have to hear the answer. She could feel it in the slap, which sent her reeling. Shomu beat her with the ferocity of a madman. He slapped and kicked her till she fainted. He waited for her to regain her senses before beating her some more. Then he kicked her one last time before walking out of the room. Shobhita ran into the room to see Jyotsna lying in a pool of blood. She sent for the doctor as she tried her best to revive the girl.

It was a fortnight before Jyotsna could stand up and take a few steps. Her face was still swollen and every part of her body still hurt, but luckily no bones were broken. The doctor paid a visit every day. The medicines along with Shobhita's ministrations had worked and Jyotsna was slowly on the mend. The past fortnight had taught her many things. While she had lain battered and bruised, her mind had been working overtime.

When the doctor came to see her next, Jyotsna held her hand.

'Can you please come with me, Didi?'

'You are in no position to move, Jyotsna,' the doctor said.

But Jyotsna was adamant. She was barely able to walk, but she insisted on being taken out. the doctor had never seen her like this before, so she complied quietly.

Jyotsna limped into the doctor's car and spoke in a clear voice, 'Please take me to the police station.'

'Jyotsna, are you sure this is what you want to do? The Chatterjees are extremely powerful people. The police might not even lodge a complaint. Also, you will get me into trouble.'

'You have helped me so much, Didi. Please help me a bit more. I have kept quiet all this while. I worried about my mother and my son, but I won't be cowed down anymore. If the policemen here don't listen to me, I'll take my complaint to Kolkata. I will do everything I can to expose this monstrous duo. I have lived in fear far too long.'

'But your son, Jyotsna? He's with them. You might never get to see him.'

'My mother has lived without seeing me for this long, Didi. I will get my son back one day. It's going to be a long battle, Didi, but I'll fight. Will you help me?'

The doctor was speechless. She had known Jyotsna for a long time. The girl she knew had been quiet and docile who smiled more than she spoke. She had seen her suffering a brute of a husband without complaining. This was a new person. Someone who wanted to right every wrong and was ready to fight for it. The doctor wasn't sure how this would pan out, but she was too fond of Jyotsna to let her down when she needed her the most. She squeezed the girl's hand and instructed her driver, 'First pick up her mother and then drive us to the police station.'

Jyotsna smiled through her bruised lips. Every pore in her body was hurting. The thought of being separated from her son gnawed away at her heart, but something told her she was finally on the right track. She would start by lodging a complaint of wife-beating against her husband. Doctor Didi and Shobhita would be her witnesses. The only way she would ever be free would be if she fought her own battle. There was no turning back now.

For the first time in her life, Jyotsna was not conscious of the eyes that were glued to her or the heads that turned to look at her battered body. She walked with her face uncovered, without the customary sari's aanchal over her head. She limped piteously, but didn't feel the pain as she walked into the neighbourhood police station.

In a firm and clear voice, she told the police woman, 'Madam, I have come to lodge a complaint, and Doctor Didi is my witness...'

10

Queen Kaikeyi

I knew her since she was a feisty little girl. We trained in martial arts together at Baba's gurukul. I loved her and wanted to marry her though I knew that would not be possible. She was a Kshatriya princess and I, a humble Brahmin's son. People had high regard for our family since Baba was the Rajguru, the teacher of the Royals. He had been hired to train Kaikeyi's brothers, the young princes, but none could stop the irrepressible princess from joining her male siblings.

From the beginning, it was evident she was superior to most students in the gurukul. None could parallel her wit, wisdom and prowess. Only I, Matanga, occasionally sparred with her, matching sword for sword, but she treated me with disdain. Her beautiful eyes barely registered my presence. Not one to give up easily, I would follow her everywhere.

It seems like only yesterday that King Dasharatha was in the forest on a hunt. Scoffed and jeered at by his peers, the king, an ageing, ungainly man who was also sick of heart, had married twice in order to beget an heir, but had failed. Rumour had it that he laboured under a curse and would never sire a progeny. If things didn't change soon, the great kingdom of Ayodhya would go to rack and ruin.

Kaikeyi's task for the day was to collect firewood from the forest. She tied her sari like a dhoti, grabbed her axe and set out. Oblivious of the king's presence in the forest, Kaikeyi went about performing her task. Her bare back shone with sweat as she sliced through the logs with the ease of a seasoned woodcutter. Every move of hers reflected power, mastery and control. Each muscle seemed to have a life of its own as she fulfilled her task to perfection. Watching her from a distance, I was transported by the sensuousness of her being.

Suddenly, the peace of the forest was shattered. People ran around frantically brandishing swords as screams of dying men rent the air. The king's armed guards had been surrounded by brigands known through the length and breadth of our land for their fearlessness and their ability to fight unto death. These men had no country or religion. Hardened mercenaries, they slaughtered cold-bloodedly for money and personal gain.

In a matter of minutes, the king's guards lay bleeding on the ground. King Dasharatha's life was in danger. My immediate reaction was to rush to the gurukul and inform Baba. We needed to return with as many hands as possible to save the king. But Kaikeyi took her decision before I could. Like a being possessed, she charged through the forest, nimble of foot, in the direction of the commotion. On seeing the king's decimated guards, she snatched a bow and arrow from one of them, and started to shower arrows on the brigands in a bid to provide cover to the besieged king.

At this turn of events, some of the king's guards got second wind and jumped back into the fray. In the depth of the forest, Kaikeyi was like Goddess Kali, baying for her opponents' blood. I too joined in from the periphery, never losing sight of her lest she needed me.

Soon most of the mercenaries lay in a lifeless heap while the rest were taken captive by the king's guards. After winning this battle singlehandedly, Kaikeyi led King Dasharatha and his wounded guards to Baba's gurukul.

King Dashratha and Kaikeyi married each other quietly at the gurukul. Baba presided over their wedding as the high priest. Throughout the wedding, Kaikeyi remained aloof as if it wasn't she who was marrying the decrepit king. For their first union, Kaikeyi left for the forest with only King Dasharatha, her husband, while his guards stayed back at the gurukul to recuperate. Mad with jealously, I decided to follow the newly married couple into the forest, but had to eventually make peace with the fact that fate had ordained Kaikeyi to be King Dasaratha's queen.

Soon thereafter, I left the gurukul for the harsh mountains, ostensibly to pursue a higher form of asceticism, but if truth be told, I wanted to mortify my body and soul for wanting Kaikeyi, now Queen of Ayodhya, so desperately.

Years went by. I trained my mind to focus on the Almighty. My penances grew increasingly rigorous. I ate fresh berries and fruit once a day, slept bare-bodied on the mountain's unyielding hardness, braved icy winds and practised archery at high altitudes. I finally learnt to live without Kaikeyi. Or so it seemed.

My penances earned me respect; I was now revered as Maharishi or great ascetic. Rishis from various gurukuls beseeched me to share my knowledge with them. Once in a while, I travelled to the realm of human beings.

During one of my travels, I found myself on the banks of River Saraswati. I thought of my friend

Vashishtha who had been requesting me to visit his gurukul that was close by. As I stood by the serene river, admiring the pristine surroundings, I beheld a young blindfolded mother, her arms outstretched, with her four sons running around calling out to her. Identifying each child by his voice, she would chase him till another child called out to distract her. From her indulgent laughter, it was evident she was pretending her sons were getting the better of her.

The boys laughed in merriment as they kept calling out to her. The river and the forest appeared to join these five in their game of blind woman's buff. I stood on the bank, watching them.

A dark and handsome young boy ran past me, calling out to his mother. With a smile on her face, she ran after him. 'I will certainly catch you this time, Rama,' she said as she ran towards her eldest son and finally held him in a tight embrace. I watched with amusement till it dawned on me that Rama's mother was none other than Queen Kaikeyi.

She was the same as I remembered her—regal, haughty and hauntingly beautiful. Motherhood had softened her as a person, but the cuts and nicks on her taut, muscular body spoke of the rigours of her training as the warrior queen of Ayodhya.

I bowed and greeted her with folded hands, 'Namaskar.'

She greeted me back, instructing her sons to seek my blessings. The four young boys bent down to touch my feet.

'Fine boys you have, Queen Kaikeyi,' I said. 'Are all of them yours?'

'Only the eldest, Rama...my favourite son,' she laughed.

A younger child hugged her by her slim waist. 'No, Rama bhaiya is Mother Kaushalya's son. *I* am your son,' he said plaintively. She lifted him in her arms and swung him around. I realised this was the mother's way of teasing her son. The close bond between Queen Kaikeyi and the four boys was evident. I accompanied them back to my friend Vashistha's gurukul. Queen Kaikeyi left for the palace soon after.

From Vashishtha, I learnt that after many sacrifices to Agni, the God of Fire, King Dashratha finally became a father. Rama, his first-born, was the son of Queen Kaushalya. Bharat was the son of Queen Kaikeyi and Lakshmana and Shatrughna had been born to Queen Sumitra. Of all the royals, only Queen Kaikeyi set great stores by the education of the boys. She visited the gurukul often to see how the princes were progressing. She was particularly mindful of Rama's education since he was to inherit his father's kingdom.

'I do not worry about Rama,' said Vashishtha. 'Queen Kaikeyi will watch over him. She is knowledgeable and just. As long as she is around, no harm can come to the Raghuvanshis.'

I pretended to listen to Vashishtha, but deep down, I wondered whether Queen Kaikeyi had recognised me, whether she was aware I still loved her to distraction? To school my mind and body once again, I decided to return to the harsh mountains. In the forbidding stillness of those jagged peaks, perhaps I would be able to forget her.

***

In the years that ensued, the fate of Ayodhya changed. Rama was banished from the kingdom for fourteen years. He accepted the unjust punishment with characteristic grace and humility. Along with his wife, Sita and his devoted brother Lakshman, he proceeded to the forest. A despondent Bharata pleaded with his father and mother, but to no avail. So he agreed to rule the kingdom of Ayodhya in the name of Rama. Rama's departure broke King Dashratha's spirit. Soon death would claim him.

The entire land was in deep turmoil. Vashishtha sent for me once again, but I chose not to respond. Years ago, I had snapped my ties with the realm of human beings; I did not want to engage with them again. It seemed only the other day I had seen Rama and Bharata playing with the woman they both had called mother. Why then had this misfortune befallen Ayodhya?

It was all Queen Kaikeyi's doing, Vashishtha informed me. She alone was responsible for Rama's exile from Ayodhya. Worried about her own son's inheritance, her greed for power had spelt the ruin of the greatest Suryavanshi kingdom.

I could have sworn with all my might this was not the Kaikeyi I had known. There must have been a misunderstanding, but I chose to not say a word.

Early next morning, I offered my salutations to the sun and sat facing eastwards to meditate. There is something so peaceful about this time of the day in the harsh mountains. I concentrated on the sun, blocking out all thought and focussing solely on the sound 'Om'. But try as I might, I was not able to concentrate. Kaikeyi's face repeatedly flashed before my eyes, beckoning me as it were to find out the truth. Thus did the gods will me to meet her again, in the realm of human beings.

***

She was walking barefoot by the banks of the river. The royal clothes had been replaced by the coarse cloth of mendicants. Her hair was piled high, unkempt and rough—the way they had been in her gurukul days. She smiled when she saw me. My heart started pounding in my chest again. No amount of penance could make me immune to this woman I had loved all my life. She, of course, knew nothing about it nor would she ever know. I folded my hands in a stiff Namaskar. She returned the greeting with a knowing smile on her face.

'Matanga, you have come in search of the truth. Then you must know all of us are pawns in the hands of destiny and cursed is the person who is prescient about her destiny. I was elected by the gods to help them play out Rama's destiny. Dashratha was destined to die childless. After his death, the kingdom of Ayodhya would be taken over by the mercenaries. Civilisation would be ruined. That is why, Matanga, I was chosen by the gods to intervene. After my marriage to Dashratha, I nursed him back to health. I ensured he paid equal attention to all his wives. Together, we resurrected the king who by then had been taken for near-dead. With the help of rishis and sacrifices, we also became pregnant. Peace and harmony was restored in Ayodhya. I brought all my sons to Rishi Vashishtha's gurukul so they could receive an education befitting their station in life.'

I stood transfixed, hanging on to every word Queen Kaikeyi uttered. Her voice did not betray any emotion as she continued, 'Rama is to inherit the kingdom, but is he ready to rule? Sita, his consort is but a young girl who is still to acquire the wisdom any queen of this great land ought to be possessed of. They both need more experience. Rama needs to understand and value her companionship. The threat from the mighty Ravana, King of Lanka, looms over us. Besides being a great scholar, he is a devotee of Lord Shiva. Rama needs to engage with him and learn from him. Till such time Rama's worldly education is not complete, he shall not be fit to be king."

'But why did you have to resort to such guile? Why couldn't you tell King Dashratha the truth?'

'Do you think Dashratha would have agreed to send Rama away to the forests for fourteen years had I told him the truth? Do you think Bharata, my son, would have accepted the truth? The life of princes in palaces is insulated from the upheavals of existence. Without adequate training and experience, Rama would have been a failure, just like his father. Kingship requires the ability to face up to challenges hitherto unforeseen.'

'But why allow everyone to malign your good name, Queen Kaikeyi?'

'Who can malign me, Matanga? Do you hate me? No, you don't. You have loved me ever since you set your eyes on me in your father's gurukul. Does Dashratha hate me? No, he does not. He knows I have tried helping him to atone for the sins of the past—the inadvertent murder of an old blind couple's only child. He was fated to suffer this remorse and pain. Rama knows it too.'

'Dashratha murdered someone?'

'Yes, Matanga. In his youth, the king was a great archer, in fact, one of the rare archers who could get his prey with a shabdabhedi arrow on merely hearing its sound. On one such hunting expedition, he heard a deer drinking water at a nearby spring. Without thinking, he shot an arrow which unfailingly found its target, but instead of a deer, he killed a young man, Shravan Kumar, the only child and support of his blind parents. The old couple cursed the king—one day, he too would bear the pain of losing a child.

'Dashratha is a cursed man, Matanga. He and his progeny will have to face the consequences. But all this, also because of a higher purpose and for the greater good of Ayodhya.'

'What do you want from me, Queen Kaikeyi?'

'Nothing,' she smiled. 'Go back to your penances, Matanga, and never speak of this to anyone. One day, I will join you in the harsh mountains. That is the only world—of penances—where we shall meet again. And remember, truth is many layered. Does it matter I shall be judged harshly by history? Ayodhya will still have a king second to none in courage and wisdom.'

She held my hand briefly before walking away. I stood silently, rooted to the spot, as she disappeared into the horizon. Kaikeyi had known all along she would have to play the villain in order to rid the world of the demon king, Ravana and to usher in Ram Rajya—just governance for the kingdom of Ayodhya.

I undertook my last journey back to the harsh mountains, this time never to return to the realm of human beings. Time and again, I was racked with the guilt of being Kaikeyi's secret keeper. The realm of human beings being judgemental beyond reason, I would probably do more harm to her than good if I tried to defend her. There would be the usual questions and muckraking. Even a Maharishi like me would not be spared. So I let her go down in history as the woman who wrecked a royal family, conspired to dethrone her stepson and was eventually responsible for the king's death. I let her be the conniving Queen Kaikeyi who had no business living, but carried on with her life unrepentant, regal and incredibly beautiful. I let the future generations malign her.

Meanwhile, Kaikeyi, till your earthly duties are done, I will wait for you in these harsh but pure mountains. There will be no greater redemption for my sin of silence than my soul merging with yours.

11

The Santhal Maid

Bulki was young, vivacious and pretty. She also boasted of a job in the upmarket steel township of Jamshedpur which very few of her ilk could. Orphaned when she was five, this Santhal girl had been brought to the city by Kamli Mashi, her aunt.

Bulki spent her childhood trailing along with Kamli to the houses of the wealthy where her aunt worked as a part-time maid. When Bulki was old enough to work, she started to share her aunt's workload. Soon she began to take care of entire households on her own. Like her aunt, she would go from one house to another, do the dishes, sweep and mop the floors clean, knead the dough and make a handi of rice. And she did all this unquestioningly, with a smile on her face.

Then one day, after a brief spate of illness, her aunt died. Bulki no longer had a home to go back to. That is when Mrs. Roy stepped in because she sensed a great opportunity. She offered to take in Bulki as a full-time maid. Bulki would do all her housework and, in return, she would have a roof over her head. Mrs. Roy did not do this out of any generosity of spirit. Good maids were difficult to come by and Bulki was young, so she could be trained easily.

An engineer by profession, Mr. Roy was to retire in some months. A man of few words and needs, he kept largely to himself. Early in life, he had been smitten by his wife's milky white complexion, her short curly locks and her convent-educated English. Going against the wishes of his family, he had pursued her doggedly till she had relented and agreed to marry him. His parents and sisters had been deeply hurt by his decision.

Matters took a turn for the worse when shortly after the marriage, Mrs. Roy had insisted on her husband moving out of his ancestral home.

Before long, Mr. Roy found himself in a loveless marriage, with his wife calling the shots. In Jamshedpur, he became the butt of ridicule—a short, stumpy, dark man married to the strikingly beautiful and articulate Mrs. Roy.

The couple was childless so when young Bulki addressed Mr. Roy as 'Baba', he was extremely happy. She would take care of him, cook his favourite food, massage his head and watch TV with him. Mrs. Roy was comfortable with this arrangement—at least her husband had company at home when she went out for her card sessions at the club.

Then came the unexpected good news. Pleased with Mr. Roy's work, his bosses had recommended his name for a three-month-long deputation to Singapore. Mrs. Roy was over the moon. This would be her first international travel. O, how her club mates would envy her. For days on end, she talked of little else, but the upcoming journey. Mr. Roy though was exceptionally quiet through it all. His thoughts were with the young girl. How would she stay alone in the house? He tried talking to his wife, 'Maybe Bulki can stay with our neighbours till we're back. It's not safe to let a young girl stay all by herself.'

But Mrs. Roy would have none of it. 'Have you lost your mind? You think you can trust a good maid with the neighbours? They'll entice her with a better deal and that'll be the end of it. No, no, she needs to stay put right here and look after the house in our absence.'

Mrs. Roy had figured out Bulki was very honest and hard working. Her loyalty to the couple was beyond doubt. So, Mrs. Roy lined up innumerable chores to keep Bulki occupied through the period they would be away. Bulki would not only keep her house sparkling clean, but would ensure the lawn was mown, the hedges manicured, her kitchen garden well tended, and so on. All was sorted. Nonetheless, Mr. Roy was worried for the girl, but as always, chose to keep his mouth shut.

On the appointed day, Bulki saw them off cheerfully, assuring them she would be fine and that she would take good care of the house in their absence.

**

Manik had spotted Bulki from the neighbour's house; he had not been able to take his eyes off her. Bulki had a lithe and muscular body, with an extremely slim waist. To Manik, she had appeared like a dark goddess, sensuous and beautiful. He had been mesmerised by the fluid movements of her body as she had bent down to water the plants. Pure instinct had made Bulki turn around, and her gaze met his. Manik had been embarrassed and tried to move away, but in all her innocence, Bulki had smiled back at him.

Late one evening, Manik sneaked into the Roys' home and was thrilled to find Bulki alone in the house. She did not spurn his advances. She let his hands caress her body. She allowed him to take her and reciprocated his love with equal ferocity.

For Manik, this was something new. He had known girls before—they would pretend to feel shy; there would be an elaborate love ritual; he would promise marriage, and yet, there would be no guarantee they would agree to be his lover. Bulki was totally different. She did not ask for anything—no assurances, no promises of marriage, nothing. With a heart full of love, she was only capable of giving. Manik marvelled at her lack of self-consciousness and as he continued to visit her every evening, she became the blood which coursed through his veins. They made love hungrily, taking each other again and again. It was carnal and cosmic—like Shiva's tandava.

Manik, an engineering student who was visiting his aunt during the term break, knew that sooner or later, the countdown would begin. He would have to get back to college. Bulki was special—he wanted her like he had never wanted anyone before. But Bulki was a Santhal and a maid. There was no question of marrying her. So, Manik did what he deemed most honourable under the circumstances—he left Jamshedpur without informing Bulki.

For days on end, Bulki waited for Manik at the back gate from where he would enter every evening. But he had returned to a world that had no place for her.

Then one day, the front gate creaked open, and the Roys walked in. Mr. Roy was the first to notice a change in the otherwise effervescent Bulki. She seemed to have lost her carefree laughter. Her eyes which would twinkle with mirth even as Mrs. Roy berated her, were now filled with an unknown dread. Her gait had become slow and measured. It seemed the child Bulki had abruptly grown up and transmuted into someone they no longer recognised.

A week before Mr. Roy hung up his boots after a long and illustrious career at the steel plant, the Roys became aware of Bulki's pregnancy. From the office to the ladies' club, a slew of parties had been planned for the Roys. Mrs. Roy would finally have her big moment. Everyone would speak glowingly of her contribution to the club, laud her immaculate sense of dressing, delight at her priceless garden, and so on. She had been looking forward to all these celebrations, and had rehearsed her thank-you speeches. There was no way she was going to let Bulki derail her moment under the sun. So despite the contempt she felt for the girl, she chose to keep quiet about her pregnancy. Bulki was allowed to stay on and the Roys pretended that things were just the same as before.

***

After leaving Jamshedpur, the Roys settled down in a sprawling bungalow on the outskirts of Asansol. With not a friend in the city, all three felt as though they were starting life again at ground zero. Mrs. Roy had preferred investing in this secluded bungalow rather than in a flat in Kolkata. She felt claustrophobic in a flat, or so she had said to her husband. If truth be told, she had done so to keep her husband as far away as possible from his sisters who lived in Kolkata.

In Asansol, much changed in the Roys' relationship with Bulki. She became invaluable in setting up their new home. In this quiet faraway land of friendless existence, Bulki remained Mrs. Roy's sole connect with her world of yore. But the thought of Bulki having had a lover behind her back would make Mrs. Roy seethe with rage. Sometimes she would scream at Bulki and hurl abuses at her. Bulki would keep her head down. Later, she would give Mrs. Roy a head massage and remind her not to scream lest her blood pressure shoots up.

Mr. Roy, however, stood rock-steady by the hapless girl. He tried to reason with his wife: Bulki had been too young to know right from wrong, to see through the web of deceit. In a fit of anger, Mrs. Roy had even asked Bulki to get rid of the child, but for once, Bulki had stood her ground. She had fallen at her feet, pleading for the life of her unborn child. 'It's not the child's fault, Ma. Please don't punish it. I'll go away, Ma, but please don't ask me to kill my child.'

Mr. Roy had made a last-ditch attempt at sanity, 'Let her have the child. It'll be the grandchild we never had. Let the girl stay on.'

So Bulki stayed on. As the days went by, the baby continued to grow in her womb. The old couple too grew completely dependent on her. She had indeed proved to be the daughter the Roys never had—she took care of them, gave them their medicines on time, cooked their favourite meals and was attentive to their every need.

Finally, when the newborn kicked and wailed its way into the world, the story the Roys gave out was that Bulki's husband had died in a road accident soon after their marriage. Moved by the plight of the young widow, they had taken her in as their full-time maid. Over the years, she had almost become like their own daughter.

Their new neighbours saw no reason to disbelieve this story, and the Roys came to be seen as a couple with a large heart.

***

'He looks like Kartik Thakur,' were Mrs. Roy's first words of benediction for the newborn. By then, her anger for Bulki had been supplanted by motherly concern. Bulki had suffered tremendously during childbirth, but she had borne it with stoicism and fortitude.

Kartik wrought an incredible change in Mrs. Roy. She felt drawn to him. In fact, right from his birth, she treated him like her own. The child was fair skinned, so she joked that the child resembled her, and not Bulki.

Mr. Roy was happy at the turn of events. He dreamt of a time when Kartik would be old enough to go to school. He would ensure that the little one grew up to be an engineer like himself.

Watching the Roys fuss over Kartik, Bulki smiled to herself. For the first time since Manik's desertion, she felt a strange sense of peace overcome her. Baba and Ma would ensure a safe future for little Kartik.

***

Mr. Roy took off his glasses, wiped them and put them back again. He could not believe his eyes. Bulki stood before him, her back erect and defiant, clasping Haren's hand. Yes, Haren, that local drunkard. There was little Haren had not been accused of—from womanising to gambling, he seemed to have mastered the art of debauchery. No one knew what he did for a living, but one thing was clear—Haren was feared by one and all.

School and college-going girls switched lanes if they learnt Haren was cycling down the street. And here was Bulki clasping his hand.

'Baba, we're getting married,' Bulki's voice rang out firm and clear.

Turning to Haren, an outraged Mrs. Roy hissed, 'What nonsense is this? Get out of my house right now. And let go of Bulki.'

Haren merely smirked without moving an inch.

At last, Bulki spoke up; the timid and calm girl had been replaced by a woman of steely resolve, 'I love him, Ma. Don't you remember when Kartik had come into my belly, you had called me a slut. You were right. I'm a slut and I want to live my life my way.'

'But Bulki, Kartik?' Mr. Roy stammered.

'Keep him, kill him. Do what you want with him. He's yours. But I've had enough. For years I have served you, but no more of that now. I'm off to start a new life.'

The Roys stared open-mouthed at Bulki while Kartik slept soundly in Mrs. Roy's arms, unaware of the cataclysmic changes that would alter the course of his life forever.

Bulki and Haren stormed off. He held her by her slim waist and she leaned on his broad shoulder. Mr. Roy shed copious tears while Mrs. Roy raved and ranted.

With time, Bulki's memory was discarded as a bad dream. The Roys formally adopted Kartik and he seemed poised to realise his dadu's dream of becoming an engineer.

***

On that fateful night, Haren and Bulki sat glued to each other on the bus which was to take them to Siliguri. Haren could not believe his luck. Life in Asansol had started becoming tougher by the day. The liquor dens had begun hounding him for money and the police were baying for his blood as the father of a girl he had recently seduced, had lodged a complaint against him. He had eyed Bulki for long, but had never had the nerve to approach her, knowing she was the Roys' adopted daughter.

And then one day, Bulki walked up to him. She was tall, lithe, dark and beautiful. Her body was like an arched bow, and her lips full and inviting. The way she tied the sari showed off her midriff. Haren wanted nothing more than to take off her sari and take her right then.

Bulki knew exactly what he wanted, but he would have to perform a little task for her before she gave herself up to him. He would have to accompany her to the Roys' home, and later, flee the city with her, and go to a place where no one knew them.

Haren was bewitched. For this girl, he was willing to do anything. A new city with a new girl was exactly what he needed. And when he had his fill of her, he could also call in clients. A body like Bulki's was bound to fetch good money.

Bulki sat still in the bus with her eyes closed, letting her thoughts stray. She had gambled brazenly. She knew her presence in her son's life would earn him nothing but shame. People were bound to ask questions. The Roys would not be able to prevent him from being branded as a bastard, never mind their story about her marriage and her dead husband. Yet, she was secure in the knowledge that Kartik was indeed the apple of the Roys' eyes. They would bring him up as their own. She also knew she would have to fall really low for Baba and Ma to be forced to abandon her.

From the trusting young girl who had given herself to Manik, Bulki had exited the cocoon of innocence forever.

***

It was pitch dark when the bus pulled up at its last halt for the night. Haren was snoring loudly with his head on Bulki's shoulder when the bus ground to a halt.

'Passengers are requested to get off and relieve themselves. After this, the bus won't stop till we reach Siliguri,' the conductor announced.

'I'll be back in a minute,' Bulki smiled at Haren. He smiled back as he watched her get off the bus. Her back was straight and her breasts firm. Haren couldn't believe his luck. Eagerly waiting for the bus to reach Siliguri, he drifted back to sleep.

A loud bang intruded on his reverie. An accident—someone had come under a speeding truck. People had started to gather at the spot. The crowd swore it was not the driver's fault. The girl had deliberately leapt in front of the speeding vehicle. It was over in a matter of seconds. The double rear tyres had reduced her to mangled flesh and broken bones.

Haren was not bothered. He closed his eyes and waited for Bulki to return. Little did he know Bulki had already escaped from his clutches and from the drudgery of life.

Glossary

aanchal	loose end of a sari
aap andar aiye	please come in
Baal Gopal	infant Lord Krishna
Baba	father
Benarasi	in this case, saris from Benaras
bhajan mandali	group of singers who sing religious songs
Bibiji	madam
bothi	foot-held chopping instrument in a traditional Bengali household
bou	wife; bride
Brahmin	uppermost caste
chashmish	bespectacled
chingri	prawn
Chhotoma	little mother; form of endearment for a young girl or woman
Dadu	grandfather
daini	witch
dholak	kind of percussion instrument
dhoti	loose cloth wrapped around the waist mainly worn by men
Didi	elder sister
firangi	foreigner
gamchha	cotton towel
gurukul	system in ancient India in which the disciple lived near or with the spiritual guru in the latter's house
ilaka	district
ilish	hilsa
jadugarni	sorceress
Jamaibabu	brother-in-law

kachari	office
Kali	Hindu goddess
kanyadan	literally, giving away a girl in marriage
Kartababu	master
Kartama	mistress
Kartik Thakur	Lord Kartik, known for his prowess in battle and good looks
Khala	aunt
kshatriya	warrior class
kulin kayastha	upper caste
Ma	mother
mandirtala	place near the temple; a sacred space
Mashima	maternal aunt
Mata ki chowki	worshipping Goddess Durga or her manifestations through devotional songs accompanied by dancing
Meshomoshay	uncle; husband of maternal aunt
moti	fat
natya mandali	theatre group
paan	betel leaf
pabda	catfish
payesh	dessert made of rice, milk, sugar or jaggery
phoolsajja	bed bedecked with flowers for the first night of a newly married couple
Pishi	father's sister
pooja	ritual worship
poori	deep-fried puffed up wheat bread
Raghuvanshi	kshatriyas from an offshoot of the Suryavanshi (see below) clan
rajguru	teacher of the royals
Shiva	The Destroyer in the Hindu trinity
shabdabhedi	capable of following the direction of the sound
shagun	literally, good omen; in this case a wedding gift
Suryavanshi	clan descended from Surya or the Sun God; also the clan of Lord Rama
taansh firingi	slur for people who ape the Whites
tandav	Lord Shiva's cosmic dance
Thakurda	paternal grandfather
Thammi	affectionate term for paternal grandmother
Vande Mataram	Hail Motherland

Acknowledgements

I was introduced to the world of storytelling through the stories my mother told me when I was a child. Add to that the rigorous readings my grandfather put me through. He had a fabulous library and encouraged me to read books of all genres. So, I delved into both fiction and non-fiction, sporadically. Then, I discovered a space in the household the books hardly mentioned. So from books, I graduated to my maternal grandmother's continent.

Didun, as I called her, was the queen of the kitchen in the sprawling house where my maternal uncles lived in suburban Kolkata. The kitchen always smelt divine. It wasn't unusual for us grandchildren to be hanging around there, hoping for some tasty titbits. We watched Didun cook while the other women in the household helped her. She would personally serve food to her large family. Day after day, I watched her serve the largest piece of fish to her eldest son, the second largest to the next son, then came the grandsons, followed by the granddaughters. In the pecking order, the women would be the last to eat. Neither the men, nor the grandsons, not even the granddaughters for that matter, ever stayed back to see what the women were eating, or whether there was enough food left for them.

This set my young mind thinking. Why was it always the woman's lot to cook and be the last to eat? Why did she never complain about this clearly unfair equation?

Didun was a delightful storyteller as well—she had her own inexhaustible repertoire of stories from her childhood and from the epics. But while I adored her as a storyteller, I rebelled against the notion of the 'feminine' she epitomised—a woman earning glory through sacrifice. It is hardly surprising that my stories explore 'herstories' in a patriarchal set-up.

Over the years, my family and close friends have nurtured my storytelling. So, thank you Nilakshi, Mridu and Abhay for reading the early drafts. Apala, I am grateful to you for making me believe in myself, and for allowing me to spoil your movie-going experience by letting me recount my stories in detail, at times over days, much in the fashion of the *Arabian Nights*.

Arindam, thank you for insisting I get my work published and for putting me in touch with Suhail Mathur and The Book Bakers. But for Suhail, this book would never have happened.

Ajay Mago, Publisher, Om Books International, thank you for taking a chance on me, and for the stunning cover.

Vineetha Mokkil and Dipa Chaudhuri, your constant support during the making of *The Second Wife & Other Stories* means more to me than I can say.

Abhik and Aniruddha, thank you for filling my life with bitter-sweet events, for letting me retire to 'a room of my own' and for understanding why I write the stories that I do. *The Second Wife & Other Stories* is for both of you.